Contents

Chapter 1 / 2

Chapter 2 / 8

Chapter 3 / 28

Chapter 4 / 48

Chapter 5 / 58

Chapter 6 / 74

Chapter 7 / 86

Chapter 8 / 90

Chapter 9 / 102

Chapter 10 / 108

Chapter 11 / 116

Chapter 12 / 126

Chapter 13 / 132

Chapter 1

Jungle Series

Written By LI DI

Gunshot

A story about
reunion and parting

Fired

from the

Back

Prunus Press USA

Original Title: 《书包里的秘密》

Original book by The Writers Publishing House Co.,Ltd.

This edition is published by arrangement with Prunus Press USA, through the agency of China National Publications Import and Export (Group) Co., Ltd.

All rights reserved.

GUNSHOT FIRED FROM THE BACK

Written by Li Di

Translated by Haiwang Yuan

Designed by Brandy Ding

First edition 2022

ISBN: 978-1-61612-146-4

Prunus Press USA

The Mengta Forest is known for hosting many leopards in it.

Now, a fierce leopard was lurking on a tall magnolia bailonii tree.

It was a clouded leopard.

Its entire body was covered with large patches of cloud-like patterns.

Alternately black and white, the patterns blended well with the colors of the thick foliage of the magnolia baillonii tree, serving as perfect camouflage for their owner.

The cloud leopard lay on all fours on a thick branch sticking out far from the trunk, like a snake pressing itself closely on the bark of a tree. Stretching its two huge front paws, the leopard appeared ready to swoop down any moment now. It clutched the branches tight with its sharp claws contracted from their sheaths.

The leopard's broad forehead was decorated with a few black dots that appeared like dried leaves.

Underneath the dried leaves were two beams dazzling spitefully lime a pair of daggers. They were calmly and earnestly surveying what was going on in the grass underneath the tree.

Leopards know the behaviors of their prey the best.

Before daybreak, the clouded leopard had begun to roam from one tree to another by grabbing their branches, its stomach rumbling with hunger. It had searched cautiously among the thick foliage with its unique hunting skill of walking on trees. It had been looking for a monkey or a large hornbill as an appetizer before gaining enough energy to go after bigger prey in the forest.

The leopard suddenly stopped searching among the foliage and sat down on a magnolia baillonii tree.

It spied something unusual in the cotton wool grass beneath the tree.

At first look, the grass was standing straight up. But at a closer look, they were bounced back in a slanting manner apparently after being trampled upon.

It indicates that some hoofed animal has passed through the grass, it thought.

And the animal must be small with light weight, since not a single stalk of the grass has been weighed down.

The observant, sharp-nosed clouded leopard twitched its nose against the wind coming from the thick growth of the grass.

It pricked up its ears instantly. With sharp points, they looked like two blades.

In the chilly wind, the leopard detected a very familiar smell—

The smell of a red deer!

Yes, a red deer must have gone by.

The clouded leopard was very confident of its judgment.

The spot under the magnolia baillonii tree led to a weed-fringed pool in the depth of the forest.

The water in the pool tasted a bit salty.

What an attraction to red deer!

It was because, to sustain their fast growth, red deer needed a little salt to supplement their diet of green grass and tree leaves.

They needed more salt especially when they were growing their antlers.

There was no doubt that the red deer that had just passed beneath the magnolia baillonii tree had gone to the saltwater pool to drink.

The clouded leopard knew clearly that the red deer would return along the same path if nothing out of the ordinary should happen to it while it was drinking.

The red deer can be so intoxicated by its cleverness that it may have lost its sense of judgment, figured the leopard. Since it did not run into any natural enemy along the path to the pond, the deer will think it still safe on its way back.

So, I will wait in ambush on the tree for it to come.

After making up its mind, the clouded leopard stuck its blood-red tongue out to lick its lips and nostrils. Then, it lay quietly down on the magnolia baillonii tree. Breathing in a cautious hush, it warned itself against making the slightest noise.

The clouded leopard knew that a red deer always kept its pointed ears pricked up on the alert when it ventured out. It did so to collect all unnatural sounds so that it could scurry for life in case of danger.

A red deer was best at sprinting, stotting, and running with twists and turns in a thick forest to escape a predator. It even met its predator head-on and jumped nimbly over it so that the predator did not have time to react and was thus left far behind.

The clouded leopard was fully aware that a surprise attack was crucial to take down a difficult red deer.

Be patient and wait on the tree. I'll swoop right upon it from the tree when it comes back along the same path. I'll jump on its back, break its neck with my sharp teeth, and tear its throat open with my claws.

In the endless old-growth forest on the border region, there were various species of animals, each species playing a different role.

A species could be predators today.

It could fall victim to another tomorrow.

As a proverb of the ethnic Aini goes, "Each kind of animals has a 'tiger' to fear while it is a 'tiger' itself."

But the clouded leopard hiding on the magnolia baillonii tree had never changed its role.

It had all along been a "tiger" to be feared by other animals.

It had crushed the skulls of bharals, dragged bloody carcasses of muntjacs onto trees, littered the entrails of leopard cats here and there, and even broken the wings of truculent goshawks perching on trees.

The clouded leopard had destroyed innumerous lives,

thus owing mounting debts of blood. However, this blood debtor remained a stranger to retaliation.

Therefore, it had no "tiger" to fear in this thick prime forest. Even the real tiger, the self-claimed king of the jungle, had to walk around as it was by no means a tree climber.

Among the many leopards that made the Mengta Forest famous, the clouded leopard was superior because it could travel on the branches with its short and yet thick limbs and big front paws and swoop vertically upon the back of its prey underneath a tree. Other species of leopards, however, had to jump to the ground diagonally before springing up to pounce on a prey.

A clouded leopard's swift and fierce attack could leave its prey no time to flee.

Now, the starved clouded leopard was waiting quietly on the magnolia baillonii tree, accumulating its strength for another bloody assault.

Before long, the gentle clips and clops on the grass came from under the tree.

The clouded leopard widened its eyes.

They were lit with chilling gleams of death and red flashes of excitement aroused by an imminent kill.

The clouded leopard was convinced that it would be the winner in the coming fight.

An absolute winner.

But something unexpected happened.

Coming under the magnolia baillonii tree were two horses! Not the red deer!

Each horse was carrying a person on its back.

Chapter 2

One horse was black, and the other white.

One rider was old, and the other young.

The dew that kept dripping from tall trees had dampened Grandpa Weisbu's headdress fashioned from a long piece of black cloth. He was on the black horse.

The condensation on tree leaves originated from the warm, moist air rising in the forest. The locals, however, would rather believe it to be the miasma, or "bad vapor," discharged by demons. Dropping directly on one's head, it would allegedly cause fever and chills alternately, and one could die of a disease like cholera or malaria.

For that reason, all the Hani people living in the mountain woods wear their headdresses.

Grandpa Weisbu's headdress was battered and discolored by weather.

His sideburns sticking out the headdress were also mixed with grey hair.

How could someone in his fifties who had been promoted from a dad to a grandpa not have grey hair?

One had to face it when one was getting old.

The web-like wrinkles crisscrossing his tanned face were growing deeper with each passing day. They appeared like silk threads embedded deep in the flesh. The few lines on the forehead resembled the nodes of bamboo culms.

His back was bent, so that the sling of the shining black copper rifle slipped from his shoulder from time to time.

His hands clutching the reins of the horse appeared like dried twigs, and the outstanding sinuous veins looked like wriggling earthworms.

All indicated that Grandpa Weisbu was old.

He was no longer the young hunter that had once dragged a three-hundred-pound wild boar by its tusks to the village from the bamboo forest in the mountain.

But underneath the thick, goshawk-wing-like eyebrows were flickering his sharp eyes radiating uncompromising intelligence.

The radiation was filled with keen wisdom and irresistible courage.

Seeing his eyes, one might feel that Grandpa Weisbu was not old at all. In fact, he seemed to be full of youth and vigor.

"Watch it! Gulong! Don't doze off and fall from your horse to get your nose squashed!"

Turning back, Grandpa Weisbu warned the boy riding the white horse.

"Don't worry, Grandpa Weisbu. My nose is made from sweet rice. When it's squashed, it can still be molded back."

Well, a boy is a boy after all. While his is about sixteen, he's still acting kind of like a child.

Smirking as he twitched the corner of his mouth, Grandpa Weisbu jested, "Oho! Even the birds in the Wild Bamboo Forest know that Gulong has a nose with a beautiful high bridge. If it couldn't be molded back, your mom and dad would rip my head off when we get to our Nuoda Mountain today."

Indeed, like his father Bozhagu, Gulong had a handsome Roman nose set on his oval face, matching perfectly with his thin lips and eyes as big as those of a dragon's. He was indeed a good-looking teenager.

Gulong wore a blue cloth shirt reaching only to his navel and a pair of loose pants of indigo cash. The three rows of silver buttons on the front of his shirt clinked against each other as he was heaving with the cadence of the horse. He had a distinctly angular scarlet headdress, which, set off by the hardwood crossbow and muntjac-skin quiver slung over his shoulder, made him look like a real Hani man.

When the wild loquat trees had bloomed on the mountain a year before, Gulong's parents had been transferred after many years of service with the public security border checkpoint in the Wild Bamboo Forest. They were assigned to set up a new border inspection station in the Nuoda Mountain.

Considering that they were strangers to the new location and its people, his parents had left him in the care of Grandpa Weisbu, a courier of the inspection post. Before his departure, Bozhagu handed his crossbow and quiver of arrows to Grandpa Weisbu.

"It's time for a hawk chick to practice flying, Grandpa Weisbu," said Bozhagu. "Thank you so much for taking care of him!"

Receiving the crossbow and quiver with both hands, Grandpa Weisbu slung them over the tender shoulder of Gulong.

"Don't worry! When the hawk chick flies into the sky, I'll be the wind to carry it. When it drops to the ground, I'll be the tree to catch it."

Since then, Gulong had become Grandpa Weisbu's little "tag-along."

Grandpa had started his training with horsemanship. Before long, Gulong had become a dexterous rider as joyous as a bird.

The two horses also became his fans.

The black one was named Bamu, and the white one Silu.

They liked to rotate their pointed ears all the time. No

matter what Gulong said to them, they nodded with a resonant snort to indicate their understanding of his words.

Gulong followed Grandpa Weisbu on horseback through forests of trees and bamboos and over hills and valleys. They were running shipping errands to the new checkpoint, still inaccessible by road. They sent letters and official documents from the checkpoint to the prefectural government. Then, from the seat of the prefecture they brought articles of daily use like food, edible oil, and clothes to the checkpoint. They were inseparable even in their spare time; for Grandpa took Gulong either to hunt in the forests or to help with the chores at the checkpoint.

Like a fawn arriving at a pond rich in aquatic plants, Gulong became acquainted with a lot of courageous people that he called uncles in the checkpoint. They included talkative Uncle Jielu, tall Uncle Fei Yufu, bearded Uncle Liu Bie, and the checkpoint head Uncle Ban Zhang, who had taken over his father's responsibilities.

These uncles worked hard every day, carefully inspecting the items brought by people who walked in and out of China to visit their relatives or do business. They looked for contraband, particularly drugs, contained in their luggage or bags.

Uncle Ban Zhang told Gulong that the drug-trafficking criminals were the most hateful. Some of them smuggled drugs from abroad to sell in China. Some used the border as a transfer point so that they could ship their drugs to Hong Kong and then smuggled them abroad. Fighting with these extremely cruel and merciless criminals was at the core of this checkpoint's operation.

But, these bad guys were hard to contend with.

Gulong had heard from his father many times that on the border of the Wild Bamboo Forest, there was a gang of drug traffickers nicknamed "Scorpion." They were very active and elusive. The checkpoint had been working on the case for several years and only caught a few members at the lower levels of the gang's hierarchy. The leader named "Scorpion" was still at large.

Living day and night with the uncles at the checkpoint, Gulong had gained a lot of knowledge and acquired a lot of skills. However, he often pursed his lips, causing his cheeks to appear like the vocal sac of a croaking frog.

That was because he had never been allowed to participate in the uncles' operations to pursue the drug-trafficking criminals.

Neither had Grandpa Weisbu, of course.

Uncle Ban Zhang, the head of the checkpoint, had almost calloused Gulong's ears by his repeated rational:

"It's too dangerous for you to be in a combat involving firearms. It's better for you, an old man and a young boy, to stay behind and look after the checkpoint."

The head of the checkpoint left no loopholes in his decision, which he saw as a sheet of metal that should not have the slightest microscopic crack.

Time went by so fast that, in a blink of an eye, the wild loquat trees on the mountain bloomed again.

Gulong's father sent word that he wanted Gulong to join

him and his wife.

The message also said that a school had been set up in the Nuoda Mountain, and Gulong could receive school education again.

Upon hearing that he could return to his parents, Gulong jumped with joy.

But, Gulong's happy face soon dropped, as lifeless as a shriveled squash leaf. He thought of leaving the Wild Bamboo Forest, the uncles working at the checkpoint, and Grandpa Weisbu, along with his beloved horses.

Gently stroking his head, Uncle Ban Zhang said,

"Well, after the wren bird is gone, the forest will become lonely and quiet. We don't want you to leave us, either. But, your mom and dad are expecting you like grains looking forward to rainfall. Go, and to where your parents are. Behave and study hard. When you think of us, you can yell toward the Wild Bamboo Forest on a hilltop, and the loving wind will bring your thought to us."

Gulong thus said goodbye to the Wild Bamboo Forest.

At Gulong's insistence, the head of the checkpoint Ban Zhang agreed that he could complete the last task for the checkpoint with Grandpa Weisbu: sending the inventory of the seized contraband to the prefectural government. Then, Grandpa Weisbu would escort him to the Nuoda Mountain and hand him over to his parents in person.

At their departure, Uncle Fei Yufu hung a beautiful schoolbag of blue cloth over the neck of the white horse under Gulong. He had spent the whole night sewing it.

"Bye, Gulong!" Uncle Fei Yufu waved his papaya-leaf-sized hand and said, "When the mountain spring begins to bubble again, we wish it to be the echo of you reading aloud."

Gulong set off with Grandpa Weisbu.

After delivering the inventory to the prefectural government, they turned back and traveled on the winding mountain path for two days and nights before approaching the Mengta Forest.

From here, they could have returned to the checkpoint in half a day if they had gone toward the east.

Assuming they were going home, the two horses took the familiar path leading to the east, their eyes narrowing.

"Hey! We're not going back home!" yelled Grandpa Weisbu to his horse Bamu. "Turn back and go to the west. Today, I'll take you to a new path. So, keep your eyes wide open."

Upon Grandpa's words, Bamu turned around.

Silu followed suit.

They went into the Mengta Forest.

Grandpa Weisbu told Gulong that they would have reached the Nuoda Mountain by sunset after going through this forest and over that hill.

As if they had anticipated their young master Gulong's eventual departure, Silu and Bamu walked in a slower and gentler pace than usual on the narrow path covered with fallen leaves.

Crunching, crunching, crunching...

Bamu, who had been leading the way, reached beneath the magnolia baillonii tree first.

Certainly, it was impossible for it to see the clouded leopard hiding on the tree.

But, traversing the thick forests deep in the mountains for years, it had learned to be on the lookout all the time. So much so that it could discern a different odor coming from the musty fallen leaves all over the place.

An odor that foreboded danger!

Bamu pricked up its ears, flared its nostrils, and balked, keeping one of its front hooves in the air.

It felt as if that the ominous odor had come right underneath it.

The horse had barely collected itself when a grey blanket whooshed down from the sky. It was the clouded leopard that suddenly leapt from the tree, whipping up a sinister blast in its wake.

Extreme hunger forced the leopard to launch a risky attack that it had never done before.

"Raaaaaaawr!"

Bamu reared up, neighing in alarm, and tossed its head, and by doing so, it knocked a fork off the lower part of a tree.

Grandpa Weisbu gave a shudder and hurried to hold his reins tight.

The copper rifle carried on his back slipped from his shoulder.

It all happened too soon.

Before Grandpa Weisbu managed to take hold of his rifle, the leopard had gotten in front of him.

With its unique tactics, the leopard had opened its paws in the air and aimed their sharp claws at Grandpa Weisbu's neck.

A simple scratch on the neck would prove deadly.

At this critical juncture, Grandpa Weisbu dodged with a swift turn of his body.

By shifting his neck from harm's way, he unwittingly exposed his right shoulder to the sharp claws.

The clouded leopard reached to grab his right shoulder with the claws on both paws. With a snap, they got hold of the copper rifle about to drop.

Earnest to win a quick fight, the leopard mistook the rifle for Grandpa Weisbu's shoulder and would not let it go for the world.

In this dangerous situation, Grandpa Weisbu thought quickly and gave up the sling that held the rifle.

With the rifle in its paws, the leopard landed on the ground missing Grandpa Weisbu's shoulder.

Grandpa Weisbu might have conquered innumerous ferocious beasts and birds of prey with his extraordinary skills, but he was old after all. The swoop of the leopard and the jolt of his horse threw him out of balance. He fell off the horse and thumped to the ground along with the descent of the leopard that had just missed him.

The bouts of offense and defense transpired in a blink of an eye.

Gu Long, who was close behind Grandpa, screamed and hurried to take his crossbow and arrow.

At this critical moment, however, his hands trembled. Only after making several attempts did he manage to pull an arrow from his muntjac-skin quiver. The arrow had been dabbed with a poison causing instant death.

This potent toxin was extracted from the sap of a kind of trees. An arrow dipped in it could kill an animal by hitting any part of its body, as the poison would clot its blood upon contact.

Gulong put the poison arrow on the bow and was about to aim and shoot when he saw the clouded leopard swishing over and landing by a tree. It had turned toward him in the air, with the copper rifle held tight in its front paws.

Crash! The copper rifle struck the exposed tree root sideways. Its stock bounced back and hit the leopard right on the forehead.

Ouch!

The clouded leopard gave an angry growl that tremored the ground.

Not until then did it realize that what he had in its paws was not Grandpa Weisbu's arm.

Flying into a rage from embarrassment, it let go the copper rifle and turned, its eyes glaring with brightening flame of menace.

When it saw its original prey Grandpa Weisbu fallen from his horseback, it roared, leapt up, and pounced on him.

Meanwhile, Gulong was aiming at the clouded leopard's chest.

A great timing for a good shot!

Focused on a deadly battle with Grandpa Weisbu, how could the clouded leopard pay any attention to an arrow about to come its way out of the blue?

The poison arrow was targeted at its chest.

Even if the leopard had darted forward then, the arrow would have been able to hit its hip.

Gulong was about to release the arrow when Bamu raised its head neighing, turned around, and, bucked, kicking out relentlessly at the leopard.

Bamu was venting all its anger through its hind legs.

The horse did not realize that its vigorous body, abruptly raised, was blocking Gulong's view like a black wall.

Seeing two horse hooves falling upon it, the clouded leopard called off its attack and turned its head aside to dodge them.

Giving up Grandpa Weisbu, it twisted its body around and charged at Bamu.

His attempt to shoot frustrated, Gulong hurried Silu under him with his palm so that it could take him to a vantage ground.

When Silu saw the clouded leopard pouncing on Bamu, it let out a neigh as it reared up and kicked at the beast. In doing so, it barely threw Gulong off its back.

In panic, Gulong dropped his crossbow as he worked hard to hold the reins tight.

He was about to alight from the horse to pick it up when Grandpa Weisbu yelled,

"Don't get off your horse!"

Looking up, Gulong saw Grandpa Weisbu springing up from the ground, throwing himself onto the exposed root of the tree, picking up the copper rifle, and fired...

Bang!

The report was as loud as a thunder.

In the thick mist of gunpowder, there came a scream from Grandpa.

"Ouch!"

At a closer look, Gulong found the rifle already blown to pieces in Grandpa Weisbu's hands. A piece of the barrel had flown up and hit him in the forehead. Blood was oozing out of the cut.

It turned out that the copper rifle had been bent by the clouded leopard as it had struck it on a tree. When it was fired, the full load of its gunpowder was jammed and exploded in the barrel.

The loud report startled the horses and the leopard entangled in the fight.

Neighing in alarm, Bamu bolted into the depth of the thick forest.

Raising its tail and shaking its neck, Silu also dashed after it.

Scared, Silu left no time for Gulong to react. It took him with it as it ran off.

Now, only the clouded leopard and Grandpa Weisbu were left face to face.

The leopard was still in shock, quivering and staring into nothing.

But, it remained where it had been.

The previous close combats and life-and-death duels had taught it to be calm, relentless, and cold-hearted.

Not budging an inch, it waited for the arid black smoke of spent gunpowder dissipating slowly before its eyes.

Suddenly, it shook and stiffened its body, which seemed full of fury.

It sensed that it was still alive and knew that the deafening report created by its rival was no harmful at all.

It promptly turned around, glaring at Grandpa Weisbu, its eyes filled with hatred that had been intensified ten times more than before.

Grandpa Weisbu stared back calmly.

It is unwise to take flight, he thought.

The forest is so thick that the leopard can catch up before he takes a few steps.

Looking steadily into the eyes of the leopard, he kept brandishing what was left of the exploded copper rifle.

He could not do without it, broken as it was.

Grandpa Weisbu kept wielding it, which posed a threat to the clouded leopard, which could not figure out what kind of a weapon it was. He could also use the broken barrel, as sharp as a knife, to poke the eyes of the leopard should it jump at him.

The clouded leopard was wondering how powerful the weapon in Grandpa Weisbu's hands could be.

Blinking its puzzled eyes, it remained motionless and watched calmly for a while.

Soon, it realized that the odd object could do nothing but keep waving. At best, it would create another terrifying boom, an experience he had already gone through.

Breathing with guttural snarls, it was pumping itself up for another fight.

To put its judgment to test, it took a tentative step forward.

Seeing the clouded leopard inching up, Grandpa Weisbu did not budge. He was still waving the broken parts of the copper rifle.

He was fully aware that a move to retreat would trigger a whirlwind of an attack by the leopard.

He was also certain that the clouded leopard would attack sooner or later.

He assumed a combat posture in an even more composed manner. Meanwhile, he took a quick glance around him for a vantage ground.

How he wished that Gulong had returned to lend him a helping hand now. Only if he could toss him a poison arrow.

But, how could Grandpa Weisbu know that Gulong was facing a life-and-death situation at present?

Gulong had been taken into the thick forest by his startled horse and was so anxious that his forehead was covered with beads of cold sweat.

He attempted to halt Silu by pulling the reins desperately, desiring to go back to Grandpa Weisbu's rescue.

As if entranced, Silu followed Bamu closely.

Fearing that he was taken further away from Grandpa, he let go the reins and rolled off the horseback.

He fell to a thick layer of fallen leaves without the slightest injury holding the muntjac-skin quiver tight in his arms.

Unfortunately, all the poison arrows were spilled out of the quiver at the same time.

Gulong was about to collect the arrows when suddenly he spotted a pair of eyes staring at him right before him.

"Yikes!" he gasped as he looked up.

A spotted panther as big as a calf was staring at him from behind a big tree.

His heart raced with panic.

He took to his heels as he had no heart for picking up the poison arrows.

He did not head in Grandpa Weisbu's way lest he would have led the panther to him to increase his danger.

He ran in the opposite direction.

The panther had been in a quandary about whether to attack or run away. Gulong's flight, however, gave it the impression that he was weak and easy to deal with.

Without making a snarl, it darted out behind the tree and ran after Gulong…

Just as the panther was chasing Gulong, the clouded leopard was charging at Grandpa Weisbu.

It had watched him long enough.

It had simply had enough with him.

With a mighty roar, it pounced on Grandpa Weisbu like a palm tree falling off its root.

Grandpa Weisbu took a few steps back sideways, but in dodging the leopard's swoop, he tripped over some entangled vines. With a thump, he fell on his back.

Seizing this opportunity, the clouded leopard leapt up into the air and threw itself upon Grandpa Weisbu while he was falling.

With an angry roar, Grandpa thrusted the broken part of the copper rifle into the throat of the clouded leopard through its bloody, wide-open mouth. He expected it to be a fatal blow.

This was Grandpa Weisbu's last resort.

But, this vital strike failed.

The moment the broken rifle was stabbed into its mouth, the alert and witty leopard clamped its sharp-toothed jaw with a crunch and held it tight in its mouth.

Even having exerted all his strength, Grandpa Weisbu could not push the broken rifle any further.

Its eyes bulging with wrath, the clouded leopard lifted its huge paw of powerful claws and was going to let it fall upon Grandpa's face, when a scream was let out into the air, so agonized that it was blood-freezing.

Ow!

It came from the clouded leopard, not from Grandpa Weisbu.

Before the leopard had swiped its paw down, a big club swung in a full circle was smashed on its head.

What a martial art staff move!

The clouded leopard gave a cry of misery and scurried away for life.

A self-claimed lifetime "tiger" finally relinquished its throne.

Grandpa Weisbu opened his eyes, only to see the tall Fei Yufu, who had saved his life from the leopard's deadly paw.

"It's you, Fei Yufu?"

Grandpa Weisbu's eyes widened in amazement.

"It is me, Grandpa," said Fei Yufu as he let go the club. "I meant to shoot it with my gun, but I feared that it could have hurt you."

"How come you're here in time?"

Fei Yufu was about to reply when a gunshot came from the depth of the forest.

Bang!

It's not a rifle. It's a handgun!

Grandpa Weisbu shuddered as he looked up into the direction of the gunshot. It was exactly where Gulong had been taken by his startled horse.

A shiver ran down his spine. He could not help blurting,

"Ah, Gulong!"

Chapter 3

With the panther chasing behind him, Gulong ran through the ancient forest as wild as a fawn in panic.

But, he was no match to the pan-ther after all.

When he reached a big white-pear tree, the panther had caught up with him, so close behind that he could feel its ragged gasping.

Gulong dragged his shirt off and hurled it back at the panther.

Whoosh...

The shirt flew right into its face and blinded its eyes.

The panther roared, pulled the shirt off, and ripped it with its sharp-clawed paws.

When it looked up, Gulong was nowhere to be found.

Dumbfounded, the panther was thinking,

How could he be so fast? Did he have wings so that he flew away?

Letting out a long sigh of disappointment, the not-so-hungry panther walked off, its hips swinging.

How could Gulong have wings?

That was impossible. While the panther had been blinded by his shirt, he had clambered up the white-pear tree like an agile monkey.

He had been aware that panthers and leopards were also tree climbers.

But he had had no choice but to take a chance.

Gulong had not expected that the panther should have let him go so easily.

Only when he, prone on the tree, saw the panther going into the distance did he feel his legs trembling.

Gulong collected himself and surveyed the ancient forest around him.

It was dark, vine-laden, and replete with aged trees. He felt the pressure of chill creeping out of its depth.

Like myriad blinking eyes, blue will-o'-the-wisps were flickering faintly here and there, by the tangled bamboo roots or on the tree barks covered over with squamous moss and parasitic plants.

Gulong found himself deep in an ancient forest treaded by few people. He felt as if he had been thrown into a dark mountain cave or tucked into a huge seamless sac.

What is the place? He wondered.

Where is Grandpa Weisbu?

He remembered that when he had been taken away by his panicked horse, Grandpa Weisbu had been in danger. Gulong could not wait to get to him right away.

As he glanced around the dark ancient forest, a shiver reminded him of his shirt torn by the panther.

Looking down, he spotted it in the grass under the tree.

He slid down and picked it up.

Then, he detected the footprints left by the panther on the fallen leaves.

How about following the panther's footprints back? He reminded himself. Then, I can trace them to where I had left Grandpa Weisbu.

Yes, I'll do it.

Gulong thus made up his mind and shook the dirt off its shirt.

It might be tattered, but it was better than nothing on his back.

Holding out his arms alternately, Gulong slipped into the ragged shirt gingerly. He then set out along the path by which he had come, closely examining the panther's footprints along the way.

Rustling, rustling, and rustling.

Gulong walked on the rustling fallen leaves.

The sound was subtle in reality.

But, to Gulong, it was getting louder and louder for no reasons.

Rustling, rustling, and rustling.

He gave a shudder and paused.

The spooky old forest was too quiet.

Terrifyingly quiet.

Somehow, he remembered a remark made by the joke-teller Uncle Jielu,

"When you travel alone in an old forest, sometimes you may feel very quiet all around, so quiet that you can even hear your heartbeat. In fact, the forest is normal. You feel that way because you are scared."

Gulong remembered vividly how Uncle Jielu had patted him on the shoulder and burst into a laughter afterwards.

The laugher was as loud as the quacking of a duck.

Uncle Jielu then continued,

"In a situation like this, don't believe in any ghost in

the world. You must stop to calm down. Take a deep breath, a breath of comfort. Then, you'll hear birds sing, muntjacs bellow, and various other kinds of melodious ring out. An old forest is as normal as any other forests, and it's not scary at all."

At the thought, Gulong took a deep breath as Uncle Jielu had told him to.

His breath was certainly not comforting. It was instead a bit hasty and nervous.

But, he took a breath after all.

After what he had done, however, he did not hear any melody. It was still horribly quiet.

He wished to hear even a single twitter of a bird.

Is everything around here dead? He was wondering...

Suddenly, the deadly silence enwrapping him was broken by a sound.

An inexplicable sound.

It was like that of a falling branch thumping to the ground or an entrapped wild boar struggling in a pitfall.

What is it? Gulong asked himself.

He widened his eyes and gazed at its source.

Cupping his ears with his hands, he listened hard, trying to discern what sound it was.

Suddenly...

Ouch!

A gut-wrenching screech pierced the air and gave Gulong

a chill to the bone.

It was a screech made by a person.

The screech echoed through the deadly quiet ancient forest, terrifying and biting.

Gulong could tell that it was not from Grandpa Weisbu.

But, whose cry was it?

What is he in this ghostly, dreadful old forest for?

What did he encounter?

Why did he give such a miserable cry?

Gulong's heart was pumping hard, and his skin was crawling with goosebumps.

He was scared.

But curiosity drove him to sneak up to the scary spot.

He tiptoed toward the origin of the horrific outcry, moving cautiously from behind one tree to another and stepping over one tangled vine after another.

Who knows? This screamer may need my help.

At the thought, he gradually came to himself, his pounding heart starting to beat at its normal pace.

He snuck behind a huge cobra's saffron tree. He had just stuck his head out to take a peep when he caught sight of a gruesome scene that made his hair stand on end.

On the clammy, muddy ground were lying two men both covered over with blood.

In fact, one man was upon the other.

They were rolling in a heap, grappling with each other for life or death.

The man beneath the other was plastered with a mixture of blood and mud. So much so that it was impossible to tell whether his shirt was black or blue and to distinguish his features. He seemed to be seriously wounded: He was shedding a lot of blood, quivering over, and panting heavily.

But his right arm was sticking up as straight as the ring-cupped oak, the sinuous and budging veins on it throbbing conspicuously.

He appeared to be holding something in his hand.

Gulong looked closely and found the piece of iron held tight in his hand nothing but a handgun.

The man on the top was pressing his left hand around the throat of the man beneath him while trying desperately to grab the handgun with his right hand.

The gun-grabbing man was dressed in the perfect Hani costume: a short, black upper garment and a pair of long, black pants. His headdress of black cloth had been pulled open, revealing his disheveled hair.

It was unclear if the blood covering the face and body of this unkempt man with a big head and big eyes had originated from his bad wound or been rubbed off from his foe during the fight.

A life-and-death fight must involve a good guy and a bad guy, Gulong concluded.

But, how can I tell the good guy from the bad?

How can I help if I don't know who the good guy is?

The helpless Gulong had but to watch the battle raging on from his concealed vantage point.

A large area of dirt had been kicked up and grass trampled, indicating a protracted conflict. Fighting quietly with matching skills, none of the two men had come out as the winner.

Gulong now saw the man at the bottom apparently losing ground.

As he was struggling for the handgun, the uncombed man unwittingly rubbed the blood and mud off the face of the man beneath him, thereby exposing his features.

Taking a closer look, Gulong barely exclaimed,

"Ah!"

The man underneath was none other than Uncle Jielu!

How come Uncle Jielu is here?

Who is the uncombed man?

However, Gulong had no time to get answers to his own question.

At the moment, only one thought came to his mind:

Dash forward!

And get Uncle Jielu out of danger.

Whoosh! Like a young leopard, Gulong charged out from behind the cobra's saffron tree.

But, to his alarm, he realized half-way that he was bare-handed.

What am I going to do?

There's no time to go back!

And the situation does not allow me, either.

His footfalls sounded thud...thud...thud!

Thud...thud...thud!

Like a whirlwind, Gulong charged the dishevel-haired man, riveting his eyes on his temple bulging with throbbing veins.

A good kick on his temple would knock the life out of him.

So thinking, Gulong directed all his energy to his toes.

Gulong did not know that his swift footfalls had already been heard by the unkempt man.

The man looked neither back nor up ahead, his ice-cold face showing no hint of alarm.

While pressing Jielu hard under him, he counted Gulong's footsteps in his head.

Not until Gulong had reached just short of three or four steps did the dishevel-haired man sit up and shot his dazzling eyes at Gulong's forehead. Then, he lost no time in freeing his left hand from around Jielu's neck and flipping it toward Gulong. With the jolt, a tiny flicker was hurled out of his sleeve.

It was a dart no more than two inches long.

While it was small, it had multiple, deadly sharp edges.

This dazzling dart fleeted like a shooting star toward the spot between Gulong's eyebrows.

No one could take a hit like this.

At the crucial moment, Jielu burst out screaming,

"Duck!"

Like a thunder out of the blue, the scream shocked Gulong, who quickly sank his neck into his shoulders.

The dart swished above his head, piercing through his red headdress.

Then, a loud bang!

The handgun in Jielu's hand had been fired.

This was the gunshot that Grandpa Weisbu and Fei Yufu heard.

It turned out that when he had changed his posture by freeing his hand to throw the dart, the unkempt man had given Jielu a chance to twist his wrist and pulled the trigger.

Jielu meant to shoot the unkempt man in his forehead. However, while throwing the dart with his left hand, the man was still pinning down Jielu's hand that was holding the gun.

As he twisted his wrist, Jielu missed, and the bullet went into the lower part of the man's neck.

The unkempt man lurched to one side and flopped askance to the ground.

"Uncle Jielu!"

Gulong rushed over.

Jielu shifted his body but failed to get up.

He had been severely wounded in the ribs, and excruciating pain prevented him from speaking without an effort.

"...Gulong, you...you've come just in time! Where's Grandpa Weisbu? ..."

Gulong told him in brief how they had been separated by the leopard and panther.

"Ahh...ahh...Well, then, you are looking for Grandpa Weisbu, too."

A smile flickered on Jielu's twitching face.

He wanted to stroke Gulong's face, as he had done before, but he could only raise his shaky arm half way in the air. No matter how hard he tried, he failed to extend it further.

Being very weak, Uncle Jielu appeared totally different from what he had looked during his life-and-death fight with the uncombed man.

Gulong hurriedly caught his hand suspending in the air.

"Uncle Jielu, why are you here? Who's that scoundrel? Why didn't you shoot and kill him in the first place?"

"There, Gulong. See how many questions you threw at me. Which am I going to answer first? As soon as you left with Grandpa, we at the checkpoint received information that the "Scorpion" drugs ring was going to smuggle drugs in through the West Pass of the Wild Bamboo Forest early this morning..."

"'Scorpion' drugs ring?"

Gulong widened his eyes with astonishment.

Jielu nodded.

"The head of the checkpoint Ban Zhang had received the information and led the other uncles to the West Pass to lie in wait. A cowboy told us that four bad guys had snuck in through the North Pass. At the time, there were only a few of us in the checkpoint. Some had to stay and look after it, and some had to go and notify the checkpoint head Ban Zhang. So, Fei Yufu, me, and…and Liu Bie were the only ones left to chase the drug smugglers…"

His voice became slower and quieter as he spoke. He gasped so hard that his chest heaved like a bellows, steamy breath panted out as his cracked bleeding lips parted and closed alternately. His horrifyingly bloodshot eyes were closed gradually.

"Uncle Jielu! Uncle Jielu!"

Gulong kept calling. He meant to shake him conscious by his arm but feared that jerking would add to his pain. He held Jielu's head with both hands to prevent it from hitting the ground in case it suddenly hung down.

"Uncle Jielu!" Gulong called out, tears racing down his cheeks and dripping upon Jielu's red, swarthy cheeks.

How familiar Gulong was with this red, swarthy face!

It had been wreathed in smiles, which had indicated that Uncle Jielu had countless jokes to tell, and the jokes had often caused Gulong to laugh doubling up like a shrimp.

But now, only three days after their separation, he was a completely different person.

His red, swarthy face had lost its usual luster, appearing as dry as bark and covered with blood and mud. His mouth that had cracked so many jokes was now shut as if it were locked.

Gulong's tears upon Jielu's face were chilled by the bleak wind.

Perhaps, the coldness of the tears pricked Jielu, causing him to come to. He opened his eyes slowly.

"...Are you crying, Gulong? Why are you crying...? Listen, a wild hare said to a hunter who'd returned with nothing, 'Why are you so sad? We examined your eyes for free and found them crossed. But, before the exam, you had thought that your eyes were matchless in the world. Don't you think this has been your biggest gain today? You should've felt happy, shouldn't you?'"

The joke put a smile on Gulong's face.

"There! That's what you should do. What's the point of crying? I'm far from being dead. Keep your tears because we may have a big crying contest. Then, you can cry to your heart's content and become a champion..."

Smiling bashfully, Gulong wiped the tears off his face.

"Gulong, you're so great that you've escaped from the mouth of a panther. If I had been you, I would have become its breakfast. This feat alone proves you're a man now, and a man must not cry easily."

"Uncle Jielu," said Gulong, "I'm not going to cry anymore. Please tell me where the four bad guys are."

"The four hateful villains are very knowledgeable of the routes and paths here. As soon as they snuck in through the North Pass, they went into the Mengta Forest. Once we started chasing them, they dispersed. As they scattered, so did we. Now, I don't even know the whereabouts of Fei Yufu and Liu Bie…"

As he was speaking, Jielu mustered all his strength and look up, directing his eyes toward the unkempt man lying in a pool of blood. The villains ran in different directions on purpose to cover this uncombed hooligan because he was carrying the drugs. I have been tailing him all along. This greedy crook would have avoided the shot if he had given up his bag earlier. He had darts and hit me with one of them…"

As talking drained much of his energy, Jielu suffered pangs of agony in his wound.

His lips pressed hard, he held out his hand and took hold of Gulong's arm.

"Uncle Jielu, why…why didn't you shoot him in the first place?"

"I had been trying not to because I feared that gunshots could bring hyenas to this wolf's rescue. Now…now that I've fired my gun, its report will tell those groping chasers and runners in the forest where we are. They will trace it to us, and they can be our people or the accomplices of this villain. They will never allow this man to have the drugs all to himself. Hurry…hurry and carry that bag away with you!"

With this, Jielu held out his hand and pointed to the right front.

Following his finger, Gulong spotted a bulging bag cast by a tree not far in the right front. There was also a trailing-pointed knife near it.

Rushing over, Gulong picked up the knife and belted it at his waist. He then pulled the bag to stand it up.

He untied the twine around the opening and peeped into the bag. Yikes! It was full of cocaine packages. He lifted it to test its weight, and it felt as heavy as a lamb.

Gulong slung the bag over his shoulder.

"Wow, I didn't expect you would be so strong!"

Jielu beamed.

Gulong grinned as well.

Jielu sat up slightly, looking at Gulong with a stern gaze, and burst into yelling,

"Gulong, don't put the bag down. Carry it with you and beat it. Get out of the forest in that direction, as fast as you can!"

Gulong kept shaking his head and said,

"No, no, Uncle Jielu! I won't. I can't leave you behind!"

"Silly boy! Don't talk like that. Go and hur-hurry up! ... When you're too tired to carry the bag, try your best to hide it somewhere, either in the ground or on a tree, as a fox hides its food, so that no one can find it. Then, get out of the forest right away and alert the checkpoint."

Extremely distraught, Gulong shouted, "No, Uncle Jielu! I can't go without you!"

With this, Gulong stooped, trying to put the bag down.

Jielu burst into a roar, "Don't you dare!"

So saying, he suddenly pointed the handgun at Gulong and threatened, "If you don't go, I will shoot and kill you!"

Gulong was taken aback.

Shaking all over, he stared into the barrel with his widened eyes, unable to make a stir.

An inexplicable wave of mixed feelings was overwhelming him.

"You! You…"

Gulong bit his lips so hard that they began to bleed.

"No, I won't go even if you kill me!"

Gulong's answer pounded Jielu's eardrums like a thunder and pierced his heart like a needle.

His ears were ringing.

His heart was quivering.

"…Gulong, Gulong! Don't be silly! Stop saying the foolish things…You think I like to be left here alone, don't you?"

Jielu said in a quivering voice that sounded hoarse and melancholy:

"It would be great if you could carry me in the bag. But, it's impossible…No way…A goat that ties to save an elephant from a quagmire is doomed to die with it. My boy, we can't both die. We must not let the drugs fall into the hands of the 'Scorpions.' Listen to your uncle, my boy. I entrust everything to you. Go! And on the double!"

"…Uncle Jielu!" yelled Gulong with a raspy voice.

He felt a lump in his throat, the features of Uncle Jielu before him blurred by his tears falling like rain.

"Gulong, I can hear footfalls. Hurry up! Beat it!"

Gulong was still reluctant.

His feet had never felt as heavy as now.

"Good boy, go! Hurry! Your uncle is begging you…"

As he was speaking, Jielu clenched his teeth and wriggled his body.

Beads of sweat appeared on his forehead lined with bulging blue veins.

Blood was oozing from beneath his elbow.

He pressed his palms on the ground while his chest was still upon it, and he stretched his neck downward so that his head was about to hit the ground…

Gosh!

He was trying to push himself up!

He was going to kowtow to Gulong!

"Uncle Jielu!" Gulong held back his tears and said in a raised voice, "I'll go! I will go! Uncle Jielu, you must wait for me to come back."

Then, he set out.

Without looking back, he headed in the direction

leading out of the forest.

Thud, thud, thud!

Thud, thud, thud!

Gulong now felt his heart being placed back from his throat and his body shedding its weight as if it had been lifted up and up.

He had never felt himself so full of strength.

He could have carried the entire Mengta Forest, not to mention a bag.

Gulong's departure came as a great relief to Jielu.

Good job, Gulong!

His chest began to undulate harder. He meant to say something in relaxation but failed.

He had but to peer silently at Gulong disappearing in the thick forest.

Somehow, an inexplicable sense of loneliness overcame him.

He felt the entire Mengta Forest vanishing with Gulong.

Nothing but his lonely self was left in the whole world.

His only company was the bloody corpse lying on the ground showing its abominable face.

Silence! Nothing but silence!

And the silence was heart-stopping.

No one knew how much time had passed when rustling footfalls came from the forest.

The footfalls rejuvenated Jielu.

Someone is coming, he said to himself.

Who can it be?

My colleagues or the drug dealers?

Jielu maneuvered himself to the back of a tree and raised his handgun.

Come on, you desperado! Come into my line of fire!

Chapter 4

Stumbling into Jielu's line of fire was not a person but a dumb muntjac.

The only defense that muntjacs have against their natural enemies for survival is nothing but their sharp ears and long legs. A little sound caught by their ears would set them darting on their lengthy legs as if it were flying through the air. While running, they can leap over tall bushes.

This stunt often thwarts a series of attacks launched by coveting beasts of prey.

Nevertheless, for all their agility and astuteness, munt-jacs share a fatal weakness.

They run hard when startled by an unexpected sound but will come to a stop after realizing that there are no chasers behind. Then, they will, out of curiosity, sneak back to the source of the stir to figure out what has happened.

This instinct of curiosity often costs their lives in the end.

This muntjac walked straight toward Jielu. Shaken up by the shot that had killed the dishevel-haired man, it had catapulted a long distance. After finding nothing trailing it, it came back quietly to see what had been going on.

It walked with great caution, raising its head to look around from time to time.

Suddenly, it balked, its grape-like eyes widening in horror. It froze only a few seconds before it gave a sharp bleat, took to its heels, and disappeared in the depths of the forest.

It had spotted a human body, sprawling on the muddy ground like a section of a tree broken off by lightning.

The muntjac's panicky flight gave Jielu a hint.

Why do I have to be like a silly cat stubbornly watching a rat hole? Jielu thought.

Gulong hasn't gone far enough and would be in danger if the dishevel-haired man's accomplices came and caught up with him.

I must get out of here at once and keep as long a distance from Gulong as possible. As Grandpa Weisbu has told us, a doe can pretend limping as if it had had broken leg to divert a hunter from pursuing its fawn.

Jielu dragged his injured body over the ground in the opposite direction of Gulong.

His body ached as if a thousand steel needles had been pricking his ribs. It was the first time that he felt so immobilized.

With each inch he crawled, he wished to utter a loud cry to alleviate his pain.

But he bit his lips tight for fear that the cry would escape between them.

—How much a doe would have to suffer to cover its fawn!

So thinking, Jielu crawled forward with all the strength he could summon.

When he clambered to the foot of a phoenix tree, a spasm of excruciating pain made him tremble like an electric shock. The pain felt like a huge machete dropping from the sky and cut him into two pieces from the wound.

Sweat immediately rolled from his forehead and kept dropping to the ground.

God Aoabo, please spare the doe!

Screaming mournfully in silence, Jielu dropped head first to the ground covered with leaves...

A snow-white bird flew over barely brushing the tree branches.

Twittering in a subdued pitch, it skimmed gently over the mud-covered back of Jielu.

When it soared, it brushed off a small pale-yellow flower parasitic on the phoenix tree.

The flower drifted down gently and landed on Jielu's bloodstained body.

Ah, how soft and chilly the soil in the old forest was!

How moist and fresh the fallen leaves smelled!

Gradually, Jielu began to feel the beauty and vibrancy of the Mengta Forest.

Like a seed germinating and a bamboo shoot breaking out of the ground, Jielu's consciousness returned gradually. With great effort, he opened his eyes, able to feel the moist soil steaming beside his cheek and saw the green foliage shielding the sky above him.

"Whew…"

Jielu took a deep breath.

"Don't forget, don't forget/The boundless land nurtures the Aini…"

Somehow, this ancient folksong suddenly rang in Jielu's head.

Indeed, the land nurturing the Aini people is their mother.

A mother, Jielu was thinking, wouldn't bear seeing his son die like this. So, she held out her arms to embrace me and let me see once again the pale yellow of the flower petals and the emerald green of the tree leaves.

I'm still alive!

I can't die!

Holding his gun tighter in one hand, Jielu ressumed crawling forward.

He crawled and crawled biting his lips mangled due to previous biting.

He crawled and crawled dragging his body feeling like cleft into two.

"…Don't forget, don't forget/…"

He hummed as he dragged himself forward with great effort.

"...The boundless land nurtures the Aini..."

Suddenly, he stopped with a shudder.

A pair of parted legs as strong as copper columns blocked his way.

The stout lower limbs densely covered with pores as visible as needle eyes and the toes spreading wide apart— all betrayed a stout man who had been traversing the wild mountains and valleys all his life.

The hairs on his legs had been rubbed off by trees and stones, and the toes on each of his feet had been pulled wide apart due to frequently plodding on precipitous slopes and deep ravines.

Raising his head, Jielu looked into a face shaped like a broad lotus leaf.

This lotus-leaf-shaped face was as swarthy as if it were a sheet of iron. On it a pair of round eyes were matched with a pair of thick brows; and a big mouth was fitted with a broad nose above it. An unkempt beard as prickly as iron wires crept all over the cheeks from the root of the neck. Ferocity betrayed itself from between the eyes, which gave a somewhat murderous look even when the man was good-humored.

Before Jielu had a chance to raise his gun, the man of a lotus-leaf-shaped face thrusted his two burly legs forward with lightning speed.

Slap! Slap! Two big feet fell upon Jielu's arms like two slabs of stone.

"How could I walk in the dark without being a tiger? I'm your frelling Tepiao, who's aboveboard and never do anything underhand. You're hunting for 'Scorpion,' aren't you? That's me!"

What? Tepiao? "Scorpion"!

Jielu's heart skipped a beat.

He had heard about Tepiao, a thug known as being cruel and merciless.

What? He's the "Scorpion"? Jielu wondered.

So he's the "Scorpion" that has been evading our arrest for the past few years?

Jielu felt that it all happened so suddenly.

He was aware that being severely wounded, he was no match for this brute at all.

He pulled the trigger.

Bang! Bang! Bang!

A volley of bullets flew slanting into the forest between the bare feet of Tepiao and broke the branches of the low-growing bushes, sending the startled birds scattering through the branches.

Nevertheless, Tiebiao's feet seemed to be rooted in the ground.

"Sorry!" Taking a deep breath, Jielu said, "Unfortunately, a fine gun has become a piece of metal…"

"Good job! You did so to keep me from grabbing it from you! I didn't expect that you were a man!" Clenching his teeth, Tepiao continued, "Let's see how tough you will be!"

Tepiao had hardly finished when Jielu felt a sharp pain in his right arm as if it had been hammered. With a shriek, he let go the gun, trembling all over.

Tepiao continued pressing his foot hard on Jielu's arm.

"So, you want to hear your bones crackling before you open your mouth?"

"Didn't I just told you everything? What…what else you…you want to hear…"

Jielu's voice was so weak that it was barely audible.

To suppress the severe pain, he buried his entire face in the soil.

"You've killed my buddy, and where did you hide the bag he had with him?"

"…I…I…"

Tepiao bent down and glared at Jielu with his wide-opened eyes, his ears pricking up like those of a muntjac coming out of a bamboo forest for water.

"Spill it! Where's the bag?"

Tepiao shifted his posture, and Jielu felt some relief in his arm.

Jielu took a few deep breaths, closed his eyes, and relaxed.

"Hah, you're tired and want to go to sleep…" Tepiao chuckled. Suddenly, he yelled in a raised voice, "I'll ask you for the last time. If you refuse to speak, I'll let you sleep here forever! Where's the bag?"

Jielu lifted his drooped eyelids slowly.

"…I've…I've…swallowed the bag…"

"So, you're telling me you're suffering from being stuffed. Let me give you some relief."

With this, Tepiao pulled Jielu's head up by his hair and raised his machete.

Jielu said, "...I really...really regret..."

Tepiao stopped abruptly.

"What're you regretting?"

"I'm regretting seeing you too late."

"Why?"

"I should've run into you when I was still well and strong. Then, I could've let you have a taste of death."

"Okay! Take this!"

Tepiao pushed the tip of the machete into Jielu's wound.

"Ouch...!"

Jielu screamed with pain.

A sneer flickered across Tepiao's big lotus-leaf-shaped face.

"Don't expect to die a quick death. Since I'm in a good mood today, I'm going to play with you for a longer while."

As he said so, Tepiao twisted the wrist slowly.

"Ouch! Ouch!"

Jielu screamed with agony, his body involuntarily contorting.

Tepiao said unhurriedly, "I didn't mean to kill anyone to commit a capital crime. But today, I'm afraind, I must change my mind. It's because you first killed one of us and then refused to answer my question…"

Jielu was gradually unable to hear what Tepiao was saying. He only had the feeling of falling into a big stone cave with a lot of people around him, and they were pounding the stone wall violently with rocks to produce thudding sounds.

Tepiao suddenly stopped talking.

Widening his eyes, he turned his head.

He heard footfalls.

Hasty footfalls.

The footfalls came over rustling from the depths of the forest.

Tepiao listened quietly for a while.

He detected two people from the footfalls.

Tepiao pulled up his machete from Jielu's wound and darted into the grove nearby, leaving unconscious Jielu where he was.

Stepping on rustling leaves, there rushed over Fei Yufu and Grandpa Weisbu.

Chapter 5

The gunshots had brought Fei Yufu and Grandpa Weisbu to the scene.

"Jielu—"

Fei Yufu, rushing ahead of Grandpa Weisbu, was the first to see Jielu lying in the blood pool.

With the scream, he plunged over.

Kneeling on the ground, he picked up Jielu's upper body and held him in his arms.

"Jielu! Jielu!"

There was no answer.

Jielu was heavy in Fei Yufu's arms, giving him the impression that his precious life had departed from his stout body.

"Jielu, Jielu! I'm Fei Yufu. I'm Fei Yufu."

There was still no response.

"Oh, gosh!" Grandpa Weisbu hurried over and held Jielu's head in his trembling, wrinkled hands.

He gently wiped the stains of mud and blood off Jielu's face with his sleeve.

"My boy. What happened to you?"

Jielu opened his eyes slowly.

He did so with such an effort as if a piece of iron were weighing down his eyelids.

A glimmer appeared in his slightly opened eyes.

The glimmer was faint, sluggish, and cloudy.

"Jielu!"

"Jielu!"

Four big eyes shone like wildfires burning in a canyon while eager calls sounded like raindrops of a sudden shower drumming on banana leaves.

Jielu recognized the faces and voices of those so close to him.

But his face was expressionless.

Only his chapped, blood-scabbed lips moved slightly with great difficulty.

"Son, say something. If you've anything to say, tell us…"

Grandpa Weisbu placed his face close to Jielu's mouth.

"…'Scorpion' is called Tepiao. He has a big face like a broad lotus leaf…I passed the drugs…the drugs to Gulong. He…he…"

After he struggled to tell all he knew, Jielu dropped his head abruptly.

Meanwhile, he stretched out one of his arms with force, pointing straight forward like an unbending branch.

He was pointing to the direction in which Gulong had

been heading.

He collapsed…

With his unfulfilled wishes, his yearnings for a better world, and the joys and woes still constantly and alternately being experienced by the living…

…he collapsed into the arms of those so close to him…

…collapsed on the boundless land.

Fallen leaves were rustling.

Cold breezes were whistling.

The boundless land that has been nurturing the Ani people is now holding its beloved son in silence.

Fei Yufu and Grandpa Weisbu looked at each other with their teary eyes.

They said nothing.

But they had so much to say.

Meanwhile, Tepiao was following Fei Yufu and Grandpa Weisbu's every move in the bushes nearby.

The cold and damp forest wind carried over a whiff of blood.

Two bold ravens had landed by the body of the dishevel-haired man.

After a moment of silence, Grandpa Weisbu stood up.

"We must catch up with Gulong. He's still a kid, and he can't go far carrying the drug. If he should run into one of the drug dealers, his life would be in danger!"

Fei Yufu nodded.

"Looks like 'Scorpion' has come to the fore himself. He's name is Tepiao, with a big face that looks like a broad lotus leaf."

With this, he pulled Jielu's body up by his stretched arm and, taking a deep breath, slung it over his shoulders.

"Let's carry him by turns. We can't leave him to the wild animals here." As he said so, Grandpa Weisbu stepped ahead to clear a path for Fei Yufu.

They set out, one tagging after the other.

Fei Yufu said, "It would be great if Liu Bie were here to help us. Well, we're all scattered, and I wonder where he's now."

"Yes, it would," sighed Grandpa Weisbu. "If my horses popped up at the moment, it would be better. Who knows where they've gone?"

"Could they be heading back to the checkpoint by themselves?"

"They may know how to get there, but..." Grandpa Weisbu said shaking his head, "but they won't go back without seeing me. Hurry! Let's catch up with Gulong first."

Eavesdropping on their conversation in the bushes, Tepiao had learned about the information that he needed.

The drugs had fallen into the hands of a boy named Gulong.

And the boy must have been heading in the direction that Jielu was pointing.

Tepiao drew his eyebrows together as he watched Fei Yufu staggering forward with Jielu's body on his back.

He decided to get ahead of them!

He tightened his waist band and, machete in hand, rushed around under the cover of the thick forest to lie in wait for Fei Yufu and Grandpa Weisbu.

Arching his back like a prowling leopard, he soon left Fei Yufu and Grandpa Weisbu far behind.

Crowded with tall, lush subtropical trees, the dense forest was hardly accessible to humans. It was made more inaccessible by net after net of particularly light-responsive vines sprawling wildly over tree trunks and limbs and by the impenetrable bushes and weeds thriving beneath them.

Trudging ahead, Grandpa Weisbu had to dislodge the saber from his waistband time and again and cut a path through the nets of vines so that Fei Yufu could progress with less difficulty.

Grandpa Weisbu had just passed a Chinese banyan tree when he suddenly heard Fei Yufu screaming, "Aah!"

The scream was extremely horrifying.

Grandpa Weisbu quickly looked back, and what he saw sent a chill through his spine.

Fei Yufu was thrown to the ground face-down with the body of Jielu weighing heavily upon him.

Two stout men in black had showed up from behind the tall banyan tree.

One had a face of ferocity.

The other had a mouth of buckteeth.

The two strong men had pounced like lightning upon Fei Yufu, rudely lifted Jielu's body off his back, and pressed him to the ground with their arms before disarming him.

Fei Yufu struggled hard.

The fierce-looking man produced a blunt-tipped machete with a whoosh, its blade glistening like a meteor.

"Still struggling?"

As he roared, he

With a roar, he placed his meteor-like blade across the back of Fei Yufu's neck.

Not to die for nothing, Fei Yufu decided to give in and wait for the right moment for a counterattack.

He stopped wriggling.

The buck-toothed man pulled some coir ropes from the grassy ground and wrapped it around Fei Yufu's neck.

Apparently, Fei Yufu had been tripped over the coir ropes.

The two men had been shadowing Fei Yufu and Grandpa Weisbu without their notice for a long time.

They, too, had been attracted here by Jielu's gunshots.

The fierce-looking man was named Bamidu.

The buck-toothed man was known as Mangla.

Like a rallying bugle call, Jielu's gunshots brought everyone in the thick forest together, both the escapees and their pursuers.

Mangla shouted grinning at Fei Yufu in the noose.

"Haha, you can die now!"

Seeing Bamidu and Mangla ready to kill Fei Yufu,

Grandpa Weisbu charged against them wielding the saber he had used to clear the path.

Bamidu smirked coldly at Grandpa Weisbu rushing over with his saber.

He did not take this elderly man seriously at all.

Bamidu was known among the "Scorpion" gang as a master of three martial-art weapons, namely, saber, staff, and twin-hook swords. He could twirl his staff with such mesmerizing moves like "around-the-leg spin," the "down strike" and the "downward- and upward-thrusts." He could flower his twin-hood swords like a flying dragon and a dancing phoenix, slashing, parrying, thrusting, trapping, and piercing. As for his mastery of sabering, no one was his match in the surrounding area.

So, how could he not look down upon this old man?

Not until Grandpa Weisbu let his saber fall upon him did he unhurriedly remove his blunt-tipped machete from the neck of Fei Yufu.

Clank!

The two cold weapons clashed.

Sparks flew in all directions as the chilling blades met.

As if his saber had hit a rock, Grandpa Weisbu felt his arm numbed by the impact.

Without hesitation, however, he twisted his wrist to harness the momentum of his saber being bounced upward and slashed it horizontally at Bamidu's waist as if it were a tree stump.

By hoisting his machete, Bamidu exposed the lateral half of his body to Grandpa Weisbu. The latter aimed his horizontal sweep right at the former's side left open before he had the time to retract his machete-wielding arm.

The move was as fatal as a viper whipping its tail.

The move was as swift as a tiger swooping down a mountain.

Bamidu, however, was swifter and more lethal than the saber.

Swash!

The agile Bamidu dodged the jabbing saber with a move known as "leaning to one side to let a pouncing leopard pass."

Meanwhile, he parried the chilling blade with the blunt-tipped machete that he brandished as fast as a shooting star.

Another clank!

The two edges clashed with flying golden sparks.

Grandpa Weisbu's hand was stopped midair.

His slashing saber was, so to speak, pinned to the midair as well.

Bamidu's machete, like an iron bar, kept Grandpa Weisbu's saber at bay.

How strong his hands are! Grandpa Weisbu acclaimed in silence.

He immediately made gesture moves of stepping back and withdrawing his saber before charging a step forward and directed the tip of the saber hovering in the air toward Bamidu's throat in a move known as the "glaring afterglow."

With a vagarious move that seemed as false as real, Grandpa Weisbu shoved his saber forcefully toward Bamidu's throat.

Its dazzling tip went straight to its target with the speed of a snake darting out of its hiding place.

With a display of his consummate skill, Bamidu made a "layout fender" move by ducking abruptly and dodged the oncoming saber.

Its blade skimmed over the top of his head like a flash of lightning.

Bamidu escaped the attack, vehement as it was.

After three rounds, Bamidu decided to launch a counterattack. Snarling and twisting his face with deadly menace, he held his dull-tipped machete up horizontally and parried the saber thrusted above his head. In the meantime, he leapt into the air like a swallow flying sideways. Before Grandpa had the time to withdraw his saber, he launched a swift kick at him.

Aimed at Grandpa Weisbu's face, the kick was relentless.

A flying kick during a battle of blades was the hardest move to fend off.

Only a veteran Kungfu master could throw a kick in a blade fight.

It was true that Grandpa Weisbu had been well trained in martial arts when young, but he was old now. By making the moves of chopping, sweeping, and thrusting, he had exerted all his strength. He was panting, and when the kick came his way, it made him a bit nervous. Only by making a move known as "sidelong-glance at a flying crane" did he dodge the onslaught of the kick.

In a hurry to evade the kick, Grandpa Weisbu nearly stumbled.

He had not expected the bold and experienced Bamidu to play his trump card: Before his lowered his kicking leg, he suddenly twisted his body in the air like a hawk and launched a kick with the other foot.

This move was known as "a kick in a kick."

Being more vehement and relentless, it resembled an iron shoe flown over in thin air.

Before Grandpa Weisbu had the time to figure out where it came, it was slammed right upon his face. Blood immediately oozed out of his mouth and nose. Thud, thud, thud! Grandpa Weisbu was jolted a few steps back and into confusion.

Bamidu charged forward and mounted a series of attacks. He flowered his blunt-tipped machete in one move after another came, intercepting, circling, chopping, and thrusting like rain, wind, lightning, and shooting stars. In a seemingly unordered manner, the moves were fraught with chilling menace.

By fending off and dodging the serial of attacks, Grandpa Weisbu became breathless.

With a big thumb, his back bumped into a tall tree.

He knew that he was being cornered.

"Bamidu, hack this old geezer!" Mangla shrieked.

Bamidu leapt into the air upholding his machete.

Known as "chopping a tiger with a step forward," his

move could have dealt Grandpa Weisbu a fatal blow, but instead the falling blade flew up again like a crane and, with a clank, bounced Grandpa Weisbu's saber more than 10 feet (3.3 meters) away.

His saber was gone.

His route of retreat was cut off by the tree.

Leaning his back against the tree, Grandpa Weisbu took a deep breath. Then, he threw out his chest and glared at Bamidu with his burning eyes, saying "Come on! Here, my chest. Go for it with your machete!"

Bamidu said grinning, "Tired of living? Hahaha! I've been playing with you. I don't have to make that much of an effort to kill an old geezer like you."

Indeed! Although Bamidu had wielded his machete as if it were a fierce wind sweeping off leaves, he had managed not to inflict any wound on Grandpa Weisbu. Many a time, the latter had been in a disadvantageous position, and Bamidu had changed his move in time to spare his life.

After his remark of ridicule, Bamidu pointed his blunt-tipped machete at the fallen saber and continued:

"Go and pick it up! Now that you've been in a close combat with me, you're really a man! Let's practice a little more."

"Bah!"

Grandpa Weisbu spat a mouthful of saliva and blood into Bamidu's face.

"Yikes!"

Roaring angrily, Bamidu thrust the blunt tip of his

machete against Grandpa Weisbu's chest like an iron rod.

Unable to utter a word, Grandpa Weisbu saw the entire world being turned upside down…

No one knew how much time had elapsed before Grandpa Weisbu opened his eyes again, awakened by a blast of cold air thick with moist stench.

He felt his face covered with wet mud, cold and stinking.

He was going to wipe it off when he found his hands unmovable.

Only then did he realize that his hands were tied behind him around the tree with a vine.

Fei Yufu was also tied to a burflower tree opposite him in the same manner.

Mangla was rubbing some cold mud on Fei Yufu's face.

Fei Yufu had also opened his eyes.

He caught sight of Grandpa Weisbu facing him.

"…Grandpa Weisbu!"

"Fei Yufu!"

"Hahaha!"

Bamidu fleered, the muscles on his hard-featured face twitching involuntarily.

Flowering Fei Yufu's gun in one hand, he leered at Grandpa Weisbu and cocked his head toward Fei Yufu.

"Now you guys are reunited, eh? As you know, even a blade of grass is unwilling to die, not to speak of a man. How nice it is to live, to be able to breathe and talk! Just because everyone wants to live, I don't want to send you to the netherworld at once. I'm going to give you some time so that you can't blame me for being merciless."

Bamidu drawled, "It's easy to stay alive. I'll let go whoever first tells me where the bag is…"

"We'll kill you if you don't," interjected Mangla.

Casting a leer at Mangla, Bamidu drawled on:

"Indeed, he's put the consequence of silence in plain English. Well, who's going to be the first?"

Fei Yufu glared his indignation at the two criminals in front of him.

He was breathing hard, revealing the bruised ligature mark around his neck left by coir ropes.

Grandpa Weisbu looked up at the umbrella-like crowns one connecting with another.

It seemed that for the first time in his life, he had seen them spreading so verdantly and elegantly, with each of its branches and leaves growing in such beautiful harmony and with such vitality to vie for the sunlight and fresh air above them.

It seemed that their energy had been pent up.

The energy of life!

And precious life!

The significance of a tree's life lies in taking root, growing leaves, and multiply endlessly.

So, what's the significance of the human life?

Grandpa Weisbu was pondering when Mangla blurted out, "Well, none of you wants to live? You've both eaten too much muting herbs?"

As he growled, Mangla pulled a hunting knife with an etched blade from within his upper garment and continued, "I don't believe we can't crush you."

With this, he went up to Fei Yufu and tore his shirt open, exposing his sinewy chest of quivering muscles.

Fei Yufu looked aside.

"Fine! I'll turn you into a dead duck with its clammed-up bill hard to pry open."

Still snarling, he raised his hunting knife…

"Hold it!"

Grandpa Weisbu bellowed as loud as thunder.

Both Mangla and Bamidu were taken aback.

Grandpa Weisbu widened his eyes and pronounced:

"I hid the drugs. Don't kill him!"

"Grandpa Weisbu!" Fei Yufu shouted with alarm.

Bamidu nodded.

He went up to Grandpa Weisbu and scanned his face with his glare of chilling daggers.

"Humph, you're a real man! So, you can't bear seeing your comrade suffer, right?"

With this, Bamidu pulled out his blunt-tipped machete and cut off the coir ropes binding Grandpa Weisbu.

"Go! After you!"

Seeing this, Fei Yufu wriggled and said:

"Grandpa Weisbu, you…."

Grandpa Weisbu rubbed his wrists numbed by the rope and cast a calm look at Fei Yufu. Then, he stretched his back to feel some relief before he said to Bamidu, "Let's go!"

The muscles on his hard-featured face twitching, Bamidu placed his machete back into the muntjac-skin sheath. Tossing a gun slightly in his hand, he said threateningly:

"If you should dare pull my leg, I wouldn't hit your right eye if I aim at your left."

When he saw Bamidu leaving with Grandpa Weisbu, Mangla pointed at Fei Yufu and asked:

"Bamidu! What about him?"

Glancing at Fei Yufu, Bamidu said:

"You keep an eye on him here. I'm going to look for the bag. If we can't find anything after we look around, I'll fix him when I'm back."

Grandpa Weisbu set off, followed by Bamidu.

Swaying his shoulders as he walked, Bamidu was secretly feeling content.

But he was not aware that he was led further and further away from the drugs that he had been coveting.

Grandpa Weisbu took him in the direction opposite to where Gulong was heading.

As he plodded, Grandpa Weisbu was brooding:

Gulong, where're you now?

Are you about to get out of the forest?

Chapter 6

The paths in the forest were hardly accessible.

Moreover, Gulong was a preteen after all.

He had been running desperately in the direction leading out of the forest since his departure with Jielu.

He had been in a hurry and on the double.

The already heavy bag had seemed to be weighing him down as he scampered.

Large beads of sweat had rained down from his forehead and blurred his eyes from time to time.

His cloth shirt had been drenched and dried up alternately.

Gulong was so tired that his legs almost gave out, feeling as if he were walking on a heap of cotton. He stag-gered on like a drunkard.

Eventually, he fell thumping to the ground.

Instead of being tripped by a vine, his knees gave way, and he fell on his face.

The bag fell heavy on his back, and he was too weak to get it off.

He was lying on his stomach the way he had fallen.

Suddenly, a flurry of gunshots came ripping through the dense forest.

As if shocked by electricity, Gulong sprang up from the ground pushing off the bag.

The gunshots came from the direction of Uncle Jielu.

What was going on?

The bloody face of Uncle Jielu flickered instantly before Gulong's mind's eye.

I can't rest like this. I must beat it. Gulong said to himself.

Grasping the top part of the bag, he tried to sling it over his shoulder again.

Nevertheless, the bag was too heavy to lift.

In fact, Gulong was too fatigued to lift it.

What to do?

He remembered what Uncle Jielu had told him:

"...When you're too tired to carry the bag, try your best to hide it somewhere, either in the ground or on a tree, as a fox hides its food, so that no one can find it..."

Looking up, Gulong spotted a horse-chestnut tree nearby with luxuriant foliage.

He cut a vine with his knife, tied the bag up, and, with all the strength he had, managed to drag the bag up the tree. He then placed it securely between two crotches and fixed it firmly with a vine.

He took a deep breath and lay face down on a crotch to rest for a while.

He was about to climb down the tree when he heard the shuffling of footfalls below.

Looking down, he was shocked. He quickly steadied his limbs and, like a lizard, pressed his body on the crotch motionless.

He saw a face, the lotus-leaf-shaped face.

Tepiao passed by the tree looking around.

That lotus-leaf-shaped face gave Gulong the impression that he was a thug.

What was he looking for?

Gulong had never expected that he had been looking for him.

If he had climbed down the tree a few minutes earlier, he would have fallen prey to this demon.

Gulong did not creep down until the lotus-leaf-shaped face was out of sight and no movement was audible.

He raised his head and took a close look at the foliage of the tree...

It was so dense and heavy that the bag was invisible from under the tree.

He then looked around and made sure that this horse chestnut tree was surrounded by a grove of orchid trees. Not far away, two large orchid trees were reclining on the ground, and they were overgrown with large patches of purplish mosses.

All of these he could use as marks to help him locate the horse chestnut tree.

After getting everything ready, Gulong looked into the direction of Uncle Jielu with concern.

How's Uncle Jielu doing now?

What happened with the series of gunshots fired a moment ago?

I must go back and see for myself!

…No! I'd better do as Uncle Jielu told me: Get out of the forest and deliver the message.

He took a different path to avoid an encounter with the formidable lotus-leaf-shaped face.

He was running by a few trees when he spotted beneath a clump of bushes a tuft of grass known as water pennyworts, which has the property of stopping bleeding.

He halted abruptly.

Wow, water pennyworts!

He saw before his mind's eye blood oozing unstoppably from Uncle Jielu's wound.

Grandpa Weisbu had taught him to identify this hemostatic herb. Besides, he had seen with his own eyes how Grandpa Weisbu pounded the herb before applying the paste to an elderly man to stop his bleeding.

How much Uncle Jielu needed this hemostatic herb in this moment!

So, he changed his mind without hesitation.

He took off his short cloth shirt, spread it on the ground, and soon plucked up enough of the water pennyworts to heap on the shirt.

He wrapped it up and ran into the direction where he had come from.

He decided to stop Uncle Jielu's bleeding first and head back to the checkpoint to deliver his message afterwards.

As he ran, he was thinking of weaving a big net of vines, placing it over the crotch of a tree, and pulling Uncle Jielu to it as he did with the bag of drugs. Then, he would be able to hide him from view.

He was satisfied with the plan.

He sped up his steps.

Nevertheless, as he approached the location where he had parted with Uncle Jielu, the sight through the dense wall of trees astonished him:

Both Grandpa Weisbu and Uncle Fei Yufu had been tied to big trees.

When a buck-toothed thug had been about to kill Fei Yufu, Grandpa Weisbu suddenly yelled, "I hid the drugs. Don't kill him!"

Then, Grandpa Weisbu had led one of the thugs away...

What?!

Gulong could hardly believe his eyes. His head suddenly swam. Tears formed in his eyes and blurred his vision.

He witnessed Grandpa Weisbu stepping forward bravely and vanishing in the misty fog.

Gulong wanted to rush over to Grandpa Weisbu's rescue.

However, he checked his impulse.

He was fully aware that Grandpa Weisbu was taking the

thug away from the direction in which he was supposed to head.

Holding his breath, he pushed the foliage apart enough to take another look at Uncle Fei Yufu. He saw the buck-toothed thug who had been left to guard him flopping to the ground and reclining against the tree. He stretched and yawned and finally hung his head, ready to doze off.

Now here's the chance! He told himself!

Charge over and subdue him!

In a blink of an eye, Gulong came up with his first action plan.

He straightened up and was about to act when he remembered how a thug had almost hit him with a dart due to his reckless attempt to attack.

Don't do it, he cautioned himself. This fellow is robust, strong, and armed with a knife. Besides, what if he's not asleep...

Twisting his eyebrows, Gulong pondered:

I'd better sneak over to sever the coir ropes tying Uncle Fei Yufu to the tree because he's strong enough to deal with the thug!

Yes, this is a great idea.

The second action plan had thus been worked out.

With his trailing-pointed knife in hand, Gulong arched his back and tiptoed under the cover of dense woods to the burflower tree to which Fei Yufu was tied.

The burflower tree was so thick that Gulong could hide behind it sideways.

Unfortunately, surrounded only by short bushes, it stood apart from any other trees.

The element of a surprise attack was to jump to the burflower tree from the bushes in a blink of an eye without being noticed by the buck-toothed thug.

His watchful eyes pinpointed from the bushes to the thug who was snoozing with his head bent low.

He hoped that the thug would sleep like this all the time.

He slipped into a clump of small-leafed bushes.

The trunks of the bushes were tall and thin, with vines hanging entangled between them.

Through this clump, he would be able to sneak into the clump of bushes behind Fei Yufu.

Suddenly, a ripe fruit berry dropped from the burflower tree.

Flop—

The fruit berry fell into the thick leaves and made a soft sound.

To his surprise, the head-hanging, buck-toothed thug unexpectedly sprang up.

Jeeze! He had not been sleeping at all!

He fixed his bulging eyes at Fei Yufu.

Gulong felt as if his heart had stopped beating.

He huddled in the bushes burying his head in the thick foliage, motionless.

Crunching, crunching, and crunching.

The buck-toothed thug paced on the fallen leaves.

Cocking his head to look with one eye from behind the foliage, Gulong saw him walking around Fei Yufu once and threw a few glances at the bushes.

"So, you wanna escape?" asked the buck-toothed.

Fei Yufu ignored him.

Seemingly embarrassed, the buck-toothed gave Fei Yufu a kick and walked on.

He headed toward a "shoulder-pole vine" hung intertwining with the boughs of a tree and cut it into two with his knife.

A "shoulder-pole vine" is a Chinese name for Tetrastigma planicaule and derives from its shape. Its pith is filled with refreshing drinkable sap.

All those who make a living in the forest know that the vine can be used as a water tab.

The buck-toothed held one half of the vine up and bent his neck back to guzzle the sap streaming from the pith, his throat bobbing hard with each gulp.

He's facing away from Fei Yufu at the moment, said Gulong to himself.

If I jump to the burflower tree from the bushes and attack him, he can't notice me.

But no!

After drinking a little while, the buck-toothed stopped to gaze at Fei Yufu for a while before resuming drinking a few more mouthfuls.

But he never let down his guard.

Gulong scratched his head.

He found it necessary to play a trick to divert his attention.

He resorted to his third action plan.

He rose furtively and hung the parcel of hemostatic herbs on a small-leafed bush plant, on which there was a very thin vine winding all the way to the end of the bush clump.

Gulong crawled on his stomach toward the clump along the vine.

After slipping into the bush clump, Gulong pulled the vine forcefully with both hands.

The vine bent the small-leafed bush plant down.

Gulong then let go the vine abruptly.

Rustling!

The bush plant was bounced back straight, and while it was swaying, it was rustling as if someone had bumped it.

The shirt parcel was swaying back and forth with the plant.

Hearing the unusual sound, the buck-toothed let go the "shoulder-pole vine" and walked toward the swaying plant.

Through the thick foliage and the intertwining vines, he vaguely saw something dark blue, very much like a headwear, swinging.

Meanwhile, Gulong had pulled himself out of the bushes and hid behind the burflower tree without incident. He then got hold of Fei Yufu's big hands.

"Uncle Fei Yufu, it's me, Gulong!"

He whispered, his heart pounding so hard that it could jump out of his mouth.

Uncle Fei Yufu grabbed Gulong's young hands and held them firmly.

Gulong worked to cut the coir ropes.

When he found out what was hanging from the small-leafed plant, the buck-toothed thug gave a panicky cry.

But his revelation came too late.

Gulong had severed the last of the coir ropes.

Fei Yufu appeared as a wrathful leopard unleashed from the tree.

Seeing the tables turned, the buck-toothed thug scrambled to take flight.

"See where you can run!"

While screaming, Fei Yufu pounced upon him like a bird of prey.

Gulong followed closely.

He had just scampered a few steps when his legs gave in under him, and he fell flat on his face.

He had been tripped.

He felt that he did not fall on the ground, but on someone.

Looking down, he exclaimed with surprise.

"Aah—"

Lying there facing up was no other than Uncle Jielu.

"Uncle Jielu! Uncle Jielu!" Gulong called out, "I'm Gulong. I've brought you water pennyworts!"

There was no response.

Uncle Jielu appeared to be sleeping.

In fact, he was. He was sleeping forever.

"Uncle Jielu! Uncle Jielu..."

Gulong could no long contain himself and burst into a violent cry.

Indeed, how much grief could a child like him cope with?

The shirt parcel with the hemostatic herbs in it was gently swaying from the bush plant.

Gulong's tears dampened the bloodstained shirt on Jielu.

Suddenly, someone came over.

He thought it was Uncle Fei Yufu.

However, before he could look up, a big rough hand covered his mouth like a pair of iron tongs.

Gulong could not cry out.

He struggled, trying hard to raise his head.

He caught sight of a face—

A big lotus-leaf-shaped face!

Chapter 7

Gulong was familiar with this big lotus-leaf-shaped face.

"Hehehe!"

Tepiao chuckled hideously, and his chuckles were deep and horrifying.

His face was alive with glee because he accidentally bumped into the boy that he had been looking for.

Gulong's heart thumped hard.

Tepiao's rough hand suddenly jerked upward, causing Gulong to shudder with pain.

Tepie then released his grip on Gulong's neck.

Gulong could not speak.

Tepiao had dislocated his lower jaw.

Then, Tepiao quickly picked up Gulong with both his rough hands and tucked him level under his arm like a hawk catching a chick.

He darted into the depth of the dense woods.

He had scurried among the trees for quite a while before pausing at a cobra's saffron tree.

He loosened his arm and dropped Gulong to the ground.

Without waiting Gulong to stir, Tepiao had already set his big foot on his chest.

Gulong immediately felt short of breath.

Tepiao stooped down and pressed Gulong's forehead with one hand, and gripped his lower jaw with the other. Jer-king his hands upward, he put it back to its original location.

But he did not remove his rough hand over Gulong's chin. Instead, he slid it down to his throat.

"Listen! You must be honest with me when you answer my questions!"

Gulong gasped in the fresh air of the forest filing sensing that the big foot upon his chest lightened its weight.

"Spill it. Where's the bag?"

Feigning innocent, Gulong blinked his eyes and asked, "What bag?"

Tepiao was so angered that his eyes nearly popped out.

"Okay, you dare to pretend! It's a sure thing that you carried the bag with you. You think I don't know?"

His remark hit Gulong like shards of tiles and bricks.

Gulong was so stunned that he was at a loss what to say.

"Spill it! Where did you hide the bag?"

Gulong bit his lips and clammed up.

"Well, you wanna burn your fingers?"

With that, Tepiao pulled his machete from the sash over his waist and, brandishing its gleaming blade before Gulong, said, "I bet you know what this is!"

Gulong closed his eyes.

He saw Uncle Jielu's swarthy face in his mind's eye.

He seemed to hear Uncle Jielu saying, "Gulong, my good boy. Don't tell them!"

Following Uncle Jielu's, there came another familiar voice, "Gulong, listen to Uncle Jielu. Don't tell them!"

How familiar the voice was!

It was Father's voice.

His father that he had been missing so much seemed to appear before him with his dark brows, sparkling eyes, high-bridged nose, and distinctly outlined mouth...

Just then, a voice rang by his ears as loud as a thunder:

"I hid the drugs. Don't kill him!"

With the roar, the image of Grandpa Weisbu standing up to Bamidu's gun flashed before his mind's eye:

Wind was ruffling his greyed sideburns.

He stood raising his head high, his face smeared with blood and mud.

How heroic Grandpa Weisbu was!

A tide of passion, courage, and eruptible power mixed with a torrent of hot, impulsive, and tumbling blood surged from the bottom of Gulong's heart.

He blurted out:

"I hid the drugs!"

The tone and vigor exactly resembled those of Grandpa Weisbu's.

Tepiao was stupefied briefly and then said,

"Well, well! I know it's you. So, where'd you hide it?"

Throwing out his chest, Gulong said, "I've hiden them in my heart! You'll never find them!"

Tepiao's wrath almost pumped his blood out of his eyes.

Now, gunshots rang in the dense woods.

The gunshots were not far away from Tepiao.

He hit Gulong hard on his head with the hilt of his machete and knocked him out. He then directed his eyes toward the source of the gunshots.

Chapter 8

The gunshots came from the direction of Grandpa Weisbu and Bamidu.

Misleading Bamidu, Grandpa Weisbu had been milling around in the forest.

Not knowing where the drugs were, he had had no destination in mind.

Trudging in the forest aimlessly, he was looking for a chance either to shake off or to get rid of Bamidu.

But Bamidu would not give him the opportunity. He followed Grandpa Weisbu neither too far nor too close but pointing his gun at his back all the time.

Grandpa Weisbu grew a bit anxious, as he could not take Bamidu any further. If so, Bamidu would become suspicious because they had wandered far enough.

Grandpa Weisbu suddenly spotted a thick and tall kassod tree.

It had a big hole in its trunk.

Suddenly, Bamidu broke the silence, saying, "Stop! I'm not here with you for sightseeing!"

"We've crossed nineteen mountains; are we going to grudge us the effort to get over a small bump?"

"I know what you mean by your little bump! You've been misleading me around and looking for an opportunity to get away. Right? Now I demand that you go back at once."

"No, you're wrong. See that kassod tree there?"

Surprised, Bamidu strained his neck to peer at it.

He saw that kassod tree.

No doubt, he also saw the big hole.

Tilting his head toward it, he asked, "You mean the bag is hidden in that hole?"

Grandpa Weisbu nodded, saying, "You really have a good eyesight. Do you want me to get into it or you yourself?"

Bamidu said twitching his mouth, "You're going to throw a rock at me when I've gotten in the hole, eh? If I were as foolish as you think, I wouldn't've lived till today."

Grandpa Weisbu said, "Then follow me closely."

With that, he walked up to the kassod tree.

Bamidu tagged after him.

The ground under the kassod tree was overgrown with bushes and Tausch's goatgrass.

Grandpa parted the bushes and blurted out:

"A hornet's nest!"

Bamidu, who was right behind Grandpa Weisbu, involuntarily stepped aside.

Taking this opportunity, Grandpa Weisbu pulled up a handful of the Tausch's goatgrass and cast it into the hole with dirt clinging to its roots.

Groooooooowl—

An earthshaking grunt burst from the tree hole.

A giant creature covered with black hair crawled out of the hole as it was shaking off the grass and dirt.

Grandpa had already ducked, so that the black giant creature caught sight of Bamidu only.

Bearing its white sharp teeth, it snarled angrily at Bamidu.

Not sure what this strange creature was, Bamidu fired at it in panic.

Bang!

Not only did he miss the strange creature, but he also enraged it further.

With deafening roars, it rose from the tree hole and pounced upon Bamidu like a black-clouded storm.

Bamidu dodged the attack by throwing himself onto the ground and rolling aside. He immediately sprang up like a carp jumping out of water and scampered to the back of a big Ficus hookeriana tree.

When the strange creature lept at him again, Bamidu saw clearly—

It was a male bear.

At the sight of the kassod tree, Grandpa had picked up the scent of the male bear.

He had watched carefully and noticed dewdrops on the jugged edge of the hole.

They had been formed by the condensation of the bear's warm breath.

This clue had betrayed the sleeping bear to him.

Therefore, he had decided to get closer to the kassod tree, where he had then aroused it from his sleep by yelling about a nonexistent hornet's nest and had provoked it by hitting it with the Tausch's goatgrass with dirt on its roots.

Bears are prone to anger.

Old male bears are more so.

An old male bear had already been infuriated by being startled from its sleep. The grass and dirt had added fuel to the flames.

That was how Grandpa Weisbu had successfully exasperated the bear.

An old male bear is a tenacious fighter. Even if its intestines spill out of its belly, it will resume its desperate fight as soon as it tucks them back and plugs the wound with a clump of grass.

Its sharp teeth, its huge paws, its bulletproof thick skin, and its inexhaustible strength and energy—all add up to make it a formidable foe to its opponent.

Without a fail-proof plan and skills, even the best hunter does not dare to pick a fight with it.

Because a wounded bear would become ten-times more furious.

After dodging the old male bear and hiding himself behind the tree, Bamidu was chased around several times. As if he had had the devil's own luck, Bamidu saw the bear, apparently still drowsy, crouching down under the tree before slowly crawling back to the tree hole.

Bamidu wiped the sweat off his forehead.

He looked around but saw no trace of Grandpa Weisbu.

Well, he can't get too far since he's just left.

As he was so thinking, Bamidu tiptoed away from the kassod tree so as not to disturb and aggravate the old male bear again.

Grandpa Weisbu was indeed not far away. He was concealing himself behind an Osmanthus yunnanensis known as the wild sweet-olive tree overgrown with intert-wining vines.

It was easy to hide in a thick forest where interlacing vines run rampant.

Bamidu searched for a long while but in vain.

He was about to head back, resigning before the bad luck, when he suddenly heard unusual sounds.

Grandpa Weisbu, who could have shaken off Bamidu's pursuit, also picked up the sounds coming from the depth of the forest.

Clip-clop, clip-clop...

Casting his eyes at the source of the clip-clops through the convoluted vines, Grandpa Weisbu barely screamed—

Clip-clop, clip-clop...

Trotting over to him, who was hiding behind the wild sweet-olive tree, was none other than his beloved horses Silu and Bamu.

Gulong's schoolbag was still hanging from Silu's neck.

The two horses did not come alone. Leading them was Liu Bie, the youngest armed guard from the checkpoint.

Grandpa Weisbu had always treated him as a child.by calling him Xiao Bie, with the prefix "xiao" meaning "young" or "little."

A native of Beijing, Liu Bie was only twenty-two years old. No one could believe that he was so young because his face was covered with short bristling beard. Soon after his arrival at the checkpoint, Grandpa Wesibu took a particular liking to him. Whenever Grandpa saw him having some spare time, he would say to him, "Come over, Xiao Bie. Mow your face for me! Look at you, young as you are, the weeds on your face are more thriving than mine. No wonder girls don't want to see you." By "face mowing," Grandpa Weisbu meant "shaving." It was not his intention to grow "weeds" on his face. Only that he was too busy, and besides they were growing too fast. For that matter, his mother had often been nagging his father at home for his unkempt whiskers.

In his pursuit of the four drug traffickers, Liu Bie lost contact with Jie Lu and Fei Yufu.

While looking for them, he had run into startled Silu and Bamu.

He had wondered why they had been here instead of taking Grandpa Weisbu and Gulong to the Nuoda Mountain.

After he hurriedly stopped Silu, the horse Bamu also quit running.

Liu Bie was taking them on a path leading out of the forest. He wanted to take them out first so that he could decide on what to do next.

He had not expected that a gun be pointed at him from a grove.

While searching for Grandpa Weisbu, Bamidu had chanced to spot Liu Bie.

To kill him with a single bullet, he held his gun with both hands, waiting for him to approach nearer.

Passing by a wild loquat tree, Liu Bie was now only a dozen steps away from the muzzle.

Bamidu pulled the trigger...

Bang!

He fired his gun.

But the bullet flew to the sky.

The moment he was pulling the trigger, Grandpa Weisbu had dashed out of his hideout in the grove and bumped the barrel up with his arm so that the muzzle had been pointed upward.

Enraged, Bamidu turned around and fired again.

This time, his shot hit the ground.

With both his hands, Grandpa Weisbu had grabbed Bamidu's gun-holding hand and forced it to point to the ground.

Before Bamidu had time to fire again, Liu Bie had jabbed his handgun at his head.

The strike resulted in a big bump on Bamidu's head.

"Don't move!"

Liu Bie's demand was as powerful as unequivocal.

Bamidu collapsed to the ground.

He knew that he was in an inferior position facing two opponents at the same time.

Grandpa Weisbu wrung the gun from Bamidu's hand, jamming the gun muzzle against his temple, and placing his forefinger below the trigger guard.

"Grandpa Weisbu!"

Grandpa Weisbu said, as his hand trembling, "Xiao Bie, let me avenge Jielu's death."

After he learned about Jielu's death and that Fei Yufu was still being tied to a tree now, Liu Bie was indignant as well. He hurriedly tethered the horses to a tree.

"Grandpa Weisbu, let's hurry and go to rescue Fei Yufu!"

Pointing at Bamidu, Grandpa Weisbu asked, "What about him?"

Let's tie him to a tree and deal with him when we're back."

Grandpa Weisbu shook his head, saying, "No, we can't. It's not safe to leave him tied here. Besides, we must keep the tethered horses away from preying leopards. How about you staying here to watch him and the horses while I'll go to Fei Yufu's recue?"

With that, he shook the gun in his hand and said, "The thug over there only has a machete. I can handle him."

Without listening to what Liu Bie would say, Grandpa Weisbu turned and left.

Liu Bie did not stop him, knowing his hot temper too well.

Grandpa Weisbu trotted along the path he had come from.

An experienced hunter, he could never lose his bearings in a forest.

Sure enough, he located the exact burflower tree.

But he found no one there.

Both Fei Yufu and Mangla were absent.

Grandpa Weisbu certainly did not know what had happened since he left them.

Suddenly he found severed coir ropes on the ground.

Jeez, what's going on? He wondered.

He looked around but still found no one. Worrying about Liu Bie, he hurried back to him.

But when he returned—

"Yikes?!"

Grandpa Weisbu let out a scream.

Two bodies were lying on the muddy ground.

They were Liu Bie's and Bamidu's!

"Xiao Bie!"

Grandpa Weisbu threw himself upon his body.

"Xiao Bie, my child!"

With his trembling hand, Grandpa Weisbu wiped off the blood off Liu Bie's face and slowly rubbed his eyes close.

"I shouldn't've left you! I shouldn't've left you…"

Seeing Liu Bie's bloodstained whiskers, Grandpa Weisbu's heart was broken. He had often teased him, saying that girls would have shunned him, but in reality, he had known that all the Aini girls in the mountain stockades had been singing their songs of love for him in their hearts. Grandpa Weisbu had settled on a pretty and courageous young woman for him. He had told Liu Bie that he would have taken him to pick some scarlet maying azalea flowers back from escorting Gulong to the Nuoda Mountain. He had told Xiao Bie that if he thought her to be his kind of woman, he could have proposed to her by placing the flowers on her bamboo house…

Now! Good heavens!

Grandpa Weisbu wept with grief.

He had lost two finest young men in one day.

He looked up and saw with his tear-blurred eyes Silu and Bamu still tethered to the tree. They were quietly nibbling at the bark and the young leaves on the bushes.

Grandpa Weisbu went over and unleased them.

He placed Liu Bie's body on the back of Bamu.

What has happened?

Grandpa Weisbu asked himself perplexed.

Chapter 9

When Grandpa Weisbu and Liu Bie had been saying goodbye, they had never expected that Tepiao had been lurking in the nearby bushes.

Tepiao had been drawn over here by the gunshots that Bamidu had fired at the bear.

Carrying fainted Gulong under his arm, he had gingerly groped toward the source of the gunfire in the hope of running into his accomplices.

His hope had been realized.

After Grandpa Weisbu had walked into the distance, Tepiao left Gulong in the bushes and sneaked toward Liu Bie like an aspiration. He had sprung out, looped his arm around Liu Bie's throat, and squeezed tight.

Meanwhile, Bamidu had lept over like a hungry wolf and taken away Liu Bie's gun.

"'Scorpion'!" Bamidu had yelled to Tepiao, "Choke him to death!"

Tepiao had taken the gun from Bamidu and said with a grim laugh:

"Hahaha, Bamidu! That old man would have killed you if he had not stopped him.

As he was speaking, Tebiao never loosened his grip around Liu Bie's neck.

Liu Bie lost consciousness as well as the control of his limbs.

Tepiao handed his mechete to Bamidu and demanded:

"A child was still lying in the bushes. Go and carry him on your shoulders, and let's leave this awful place.

After he finished, Tepiao placed Liu Bie over his shoulders.

Bamidu was confused. He asked, "Why bothering a child? Kill this whiskered dude now so we can go after the old man!"

Tepiao said, "No wonder the old man wanted to feed you to the bear. Hurry! Go and carry that child on your shoulder. He's hiding the drugs!"

"What?" Bamidu was overjoyed with this unexpected news.

"Let's go to another place, where I can make Gulong speak!" Tepiao said coldly, "As long as he doesn't have the heart to see his whiskered uncle suffering, he will open his mouth!"

Bamidu headed toward the bushes.

Suddenly, Gulong stood up from them.

The dewdrops dripping from the branches had wakened

him up.

He sprang up as soon as he had felt himself lying on the ground.

Bamidu was taken aback.

So was Gulong, who began to regret his recklessness: He should not have gotten to his feet.

Holding out his hands, Bamidu lunged over.

He was about to get hold of Gulong when suddenly someone shouted in the woods:

"Gulong, run!"

Immediately following the shout there came Tepiao's screech, which sounded like a hog being slaughtered:

"Ouch—"

Bamidu turned around, only to find Liu Bie catching Tepiao's ear with his teeth and his neck in his hands.

It turned out that Liu Bie had remained alert.

To fend off the surprise attack, he had feigned unconsciousness in the grip of Tepiao's hands. He had done so to trick his opponent and look for an opportunity to stage his counterattack. When Tepiao had placed him on his shoulders, the opportunity had arrived; for he could have conveniently wrapped his arm around his throat. But to subdue Bamidu at the same time, he had had to grab the gun from Tepiao. Therefore, he had waited, believing that, under his heavy weight, Tepiao could not have walked a long distance before he had had to catch his breath, which would then have allowed him to grab his gun.

However, things had happened out of his expectation.

All that should not have happened had happened.

From the conversation between Tepiao and Bamidu, Liu Bie overheard that Gulong had been in their hands and lying in the bushes nearby. Moreover, they had planned to force Gulong to reveal the whereabouts of the drugs.by torturing his Uncle Liu Bie, which was he.

A sudden anger flared up in Liu Bie's heart. He pondered:

I can't let the two thugs get what they want!

I must free Gulong from their monstrous grip if that means I must give up my life!

Right at the moment, Gulong had popped up from the bushes.

If Bamidu had laid his hands on him, things would become complicated, thought Liu Bie

Even if he could take the gun from Tepiao, it would be difficult to overcome Bamidu.

Besides, when a fight ensued, Gulong's life would be endangered at any moment.

The sudden turn of the event left Liu Bie with no alternative.

He screamed to urge Gulong to flee and grabbed Tepiao's ear with his teeth and his throat with his arm.

Gulong did not hesitate.

Uncle Liu Bie traded his life for his warning scream.

Gulong took flight and darted toward the direction leading out of the forest.

Bamidu had meant to run after Gulong, but the screech of Tepiao made him balk.

"Ba—, Bam—"

Entangling in a deadly fight, Tepiao called Bamidu for help.

Bamidu swooped over, machete in hand.

As Bamidu thrusted the machete into Liu Bie's chest, Liu Bie had already taken the gun in his hand.

Bang—

The gun had been fired with its muzzle against Bamidu's head.

Bamidu had thumped to the ground.

Liu Bie had also closed his eyes.

When Tepiao had pulled himself up covering his mangled ear with his hands, Gulong had been out of sight.

Chapter 10

Gulong ran toward the direction leading out of the forest with all his might.

Gradually, he approached a grove of quickstick trees.

He clearly remembered the two large quick-stick trees in that grove stooping down to the ground and overgrown with big patches of purple mosses. He also remembered the bag of drugs hanging from the broad-leafed tree by the two quickstick trees.

While he was running, Gulong caught sight of the path winding indistinctly through the forest.

That was the path leading out of the forest!

He could get out of the forest along the path and to the road leading to the checkpoint.

Suddenly, he heard horses approaching.

Clip-clop, clip-clop…

Ah! How familiar the clip-clops were!

Running toward the clip-clopping sound, Gulong could not believe what he saw—

Silu and Bamu trotted over along the forest path one behind the other.

Silu had someone on its back.

His back stooped, the hair sticking out of his headwear turned grey, and his swarthy face was wreathed with web-like wrinkles. Under his heavy eyebrows, however, his big eyes gleamed with a sharp light.

Ahh, it was Grandpa Weisbu!

"Grandpa Weisbu!"

Gulong rushed over screaming.

On horseback, Grandpa Weisbu heard Gulong. He was as happy as a thirsty person who heard the gurgling of a mountain brook.

He hurriedly alighted the horse, tucked his gun into his waist, and, holding out his arms, walked up to receive Gulong, who was staggering toward him.

"Gulong! Gulong!"

Grandpa Weisbu cuddled Gulong tight in his arms.

"My good boy…"

"Grandpa! Grandpa Weisbu…"

Gulong snuggled in Grandpa's arms trembling like a lamb.

After trials and tribulations, the old man and the child were finally reunited.

Grandpa Weisbu held Gulong tight lest he leave him again. It had been quite some time before he let go of Gulong and began to scan this miserable boy with his caring eyes.

Silu walked over snorting, stretched its neck, and licked Gulong's face and hands with affection.

Gulong stroked Silu tenderly.

Both Silu and Bamu hung their heads down.

Seeing this, Gulong could not help shedding tears.

Grandpa Weisbu suddenly spotted blood on Gulong's head.

"Oh, my boy! You're injured…"

"Grandpa, it doesn't hurt. It doesn't hurt!"

Gulong told Grandpa Weisbu that he had rescued Fei Yufu, who was now after the buck-toothed thug.

"I see, so it was you who had rescued him!"

Grandpa Weisbu also told Gulong what had happened to himself.

Not until he heard about Liu Bie's murder did Gulong notice the body on the back of Bamu not far from him.

"What?"

It's his beloved Uncle Liu Bie? Gulong wondered.

No! No!

"It's not Uncle Liu Bie. It can't be!"

Gulong rushed over screaming.

Grandpa Weisbu caught his arm and stopped him.

"Let me go over. Let me go!"

"Gulong! Gulong!" With great effort, Grandpa Weisbu held him back by his waist.

Burying his face in Grandpa Weisbu's arms, Gulong burst into tears.

"…Uncle Liu Bie died for me. He died for me!"

"My boy! Go ahead and cry. Your tears are worth shedding!" While running his caring hand over Gulong's heaving shoulders, Grandpa Weisbu continued, "We Aini people have an old saying, 'We never blink when losing our heads for a friend.' Your Uncle Liu Bie is a real Aini man! If his relatives in remote Beijing agree, we'll bury him on a high mountain in the Wild Bamboo Forest with the most ceremonial Ani funeral."

As Grandpa Weisbu said so, a grand Aini funeral seemed to appear before his mind's eye. While a stockade village officiate, known to the Aini people as beima, is chanting religious texts, a coffin carved out of a thick timber log is carried slowly to a high mountain in the Wild Bamboo Forest escorted by a large crowd of the villagers. Wind flapped the corners of the villagers' clothes and brushed away their tears. The girls fond of Liu Bie are dressed in plain clothes worn only for mourning a loved one. Each decorates her hair with a white flower...

Grandpa Weisbu sighed. He patted Gulong's shoulder and said, "To hunt down the criminals and intercept their drugs, your uncles Jielu and Liu Bie have flown away like egrets. Their eyes may be closed, but they're watching us; their mouths may be shut, but they're still speaking to us..."

Knowing what Grandpa Weisbu meant, Gulong wiped off his tears and held his head up.

Patting Gulong's shoulder, Grandpa Weisbu said, "Nothing in the forest is more venomous than vipers and scorpions, but scorpions are more venomous than snakes. After mating, a female scorpion eats its male partner. After young scorpions are born, they gather around the mother scorpion and eat it in order to survive. Scorpions are so venomous that they don't treat each other as their relatives. The criminals we're dealing with call themselves 'Scorpions,' and they are indeed human scorpions. We must be both courageous and wise to beat them. You've done a marvelous job by hiding the drugs. We can't let the drugs fall into the thugs' hands no matter what."

"I hung it on a tree," said Gulong, pointing to the front, "Just over there! See the quickstick tree grove over there?"

Grandpa Weisbu nodded, "Yes, I see it. Good job! Let's go back to the checkpoint to inform them."

"What about the drugs?"

"The hideout you've chosen is perfect; no one can find it. Let the head of the checkpoint Ban Zhang come and handle it."

Grandpa Weisbu's voice was still ringing in the air when the grove behind rustled, and Gulong immediately shrieked:

"Aah!"

A stout man popped out from the grove and knocked Gulong to the ground with a stick.

The stout man had a lotus-leaf-shaped face!

Grandpa Weisbu was astounded and remembered what Jielu had told him before breathing his last breath: The "Scorpion's" name is Tepiao, who had a broad lotus-leaf-shaped face!

Aah! This lotus-leaf-shaped face!

Isn't he the "Scorpion" with the name Tepiao? Grandpa

Weisbu asked himself.

The man who had emerged from the grove was indeed Tepiao.

Before Grandpa Weisbu had time to raise his gun, "whoosh," Tepiao had launched his attack with the stick.

Out of nowhere, it fell whooshing down on Grandpa Weisbu's face.

Grandpa Weisbu dodged the stick with a ducking technique nicknamed "hiding in a boot" so that the whizzing stick only skimmed his head and brushed his headwear off to the ground.

Following the botched move, Tepiao immediately lifted one of his legs and launched a hard kick in a move known as "a sparrow soaring into the air."

Bam—

The gun flew off Grandpa Weisbu's hand like a young hawk more than twenty feet away.

"Darn!" Grandpa Weisbu cursed in silence. Before Tepiao regained his balance, he shot out his lightning fist and struck Tepiao's chest with a "bam."

The impact caused Tepiao to bend back. Wasting no time, Grandpa Weisbu quickly threw another punch and hit his lower abdomen.

But, instead of hitting a soft torso as he had expected, Grandpa Weisbu's punch landed on something as hard as a stone pier.

Grandpa Weisbu was stunned, knowing that Tepiao had directed all his qi, or vital life force, to his abdomen. Grandpa

Weisbu quickly withdrew his fists and changed them into claws. Then he jerked himself a step forward searching for an acupuncture point on his face that could disarm his qi force.

Anticipated the move, Tepiao used his foot as an axis to turn his body, thereby eluding the onslaught of Grandpa Weisbu's iron claws.

Grandpa Weisbu's momentum made him lunge a few steps forward.

Seeking this opportunity, Tepiao stuck his leg between Grandpa Weisbu's and tripped him to the ground. He then quickly pressed his foot on Grandpa Weisbu's back.

Grandpa Weisbu found it difficult to breathe at once and learned of the "Scorpion's" well-grounded footwork.

Applying pressure with the foot was a unique martial art technique that Tepiao had mastered.

"Since you're an old guy, I don't have the heart to press your blood out of your mouth and nose," said Tepiao as he relaxed his foot pressure a bit. "I'm not asking too much of you. The boy's told you where the bag is. So, would you please take me to it? After I get it, I'll let you go."

"Over my dead body!"

"Hahah! You all like to do this for the award of a martyr's badge, don't you? Okay! Let me carve one on your body!"

With that, Tepiao pulled his machete from his waist.

"I'm not good at this, so you'd better put up with me!"

He ripped Grandpa Weisbu's cloth shirt open, baring his leathery, weathered back.

Grandpa Weisbu bit his teeth…

Chapter 11

Seeing Tepiao raising his knife over Grandpa Weisbu, the black horse Bamu charged over, neighing and pricking up its crest.

Before Bamu approached Tepiao, a man suddenly appeared from the grove and pounced upon him.

Tepiao had to give up Grandpa Weisbu and rose to meet the new challenger.

In no time, the scene became one of flying dust and leaves.

The two opponents were a match for each other—

One shot out his fists and feet as if they were fierce winds blowing up on a wilderness.

The other pulled back his fists and feet as if they were iron towers planted on a level ground.

Between their varying kempo and footwork, they brandished their blades back and forth.

This machete of a sharp edge was lunged as quickly as an abrupt gale rent the sky.

That saber of pointed blade stabbed diagonally like a violent rainstorm scattering blossoms.

The dazzling cold steels were seen flying back and forth and up and down.

Pulling himself up from the ground, Grandpa Weisbu took a good look at the fighting opponents and found one them to be the broad lotus-leaf-shaped Tepiao. The other, tall and skillful at his kempo and footwork, was none other than Fei Yufu!

It was indeed Fei Yufu, who had flashed from behind Grandpa Weisbu and entangled with Tepiao in a fight.

The sharp-sighted and -eared Tepiao made a series of vicious movements, which Fei Yufu dodged one after another.

Fei Yufu was on the offensive with both his agile and unpredictable punches and kicks. He moved sometimes like a pouncing tiger, sometimes like a hopping monkey, sometimes like an all-pervasive viper, and sometimes like a tossing dragon. He beat Tepiao with such vengeance that the latter kept squealing for pain.

"Good job, Fei Yufu!" exclaimed Grandpa Weisbu.

Seeing Fei Yufu charging from the grove to Grandpa Weisbu's rescue, Bamu came to a standstill snorting.

It walked up to Grandpa Weisbu, stood close by him, and licked the sweat off his face.

Holding Bamu's head, Grandpa Weisbu said, "I knew you would come to my rescue. I haven't raised you for nothing!"

With that, he rushed to pick up the gun some twenty feet away.

"Fei Yufu! Here I come!"

Seeing Grandpa Weisbu bearing down on him with the gun, Tepiao panicked and found it hard to deal with two opponents at once. Taking advantage of his fleeting hesitation, Fei Yufu shot out his leg in a move known as "sweeping fallen leaves" and tripped him up.

As a tall man, Tepiao fell to the ground with a unique thump.

Fei Yufu rushed to Grandpa Weisbu, received the gun handed to him, and pointed it at Tepiao's back.

"Don't move!"

Grandpa Weisbu said, "He is 'Scorpion'!"

Fei Yufu nodded, saying, "I've also caught his accomplice Mangla."

Grandpa Weisbu asked, "Where's he now?"

"Since it's too cumbersome to bring him with me, I've hung him on a tree."

After he finished, Fei Yufu picked Tepiao up from the ground.

Grandpa Weisbu hurried to Gulong, who was lying face-up.

Silu kept licing Gulong's forehead, and as it was doing so, the schoolbag hanging from its neck was swinging back and forth accordingly and flapping gently against Gulong's face.

Grandpa Weisbu picked up Gulong and held him in his arms. From his closed eyes, Grandpa Weisbu knew that he had received a heavy blow from Tepiao.

He carefully placed Gulong on Silu's back.

Fei Yufu escorting Tepiao toward Bamu.

Bamu stared at Tepiao, and convinced that he was a thug, snorted, pawed, and forcibly stamped.

Tiebiao dodged in anticipation of a kick from Bamu.

"Don't you see, 'Scorpion'? Since you've done so many evil things, even horses won't forgive you!" With that, Fei Yufu took a coir rope off the saddle, tied Tepiao's hands to one end and fastened the other firmly to the saddle.

Making sure that the coir rope was secured, Fei Yufu looked back and asked:

Grandpa Weisbu, are the drugs far from us?"

Grandpa Weisbu pointed to the front, saying, "Right in the quickstick tree grove. The boy Gulong's really resourceful. He hung them on a tree."

Fei Yufu took Bamu's harness and said, "Grandpa, let's get the drugs off the tree."

Grandpa Weisbu said, "We'd better go to the checkpoint and ask the head Ban Zhang to come and get them."

Fei Yufu said, "It's risky to leave the drugs here. We have horses. Let's bring them with us."

Grandpa Wesisub nodded, "Fine with me."

In the direction that Gulong had pointed, Grandpa Weisbu located the broad-leafed tree in no time.

Fei Yufu climbed up the tree nimbly and got hold of the bag of drugs from the crotch.

Fei Yufu placed the bag on Bamu's back.

Tepiao gazed at the bulging bag with his widened greedy eyes.

"You're still not taking it lying down, eh?" sneered Grandpa Weisbu.

But, right at the moment, Grandpa Weisbu heard a gunshot—

Bang!

The shot sounded so sudden and close.

Grandpa Weisbu felt as if someone had thrusted a dagger into his back.

He covered his chest with his hands. Warm blood oozed through his dried and wrinkled fingers.

Grandpa Weisbu stumbled a few steps forward and struggled to turn around shivering.

He could not believe his eyes; he could not believe what he saw.

"Fei Yufu, you?"

Astonished and quivering his chapped lips, Grandpa Weisbu laid his eyes on the gun in Fei Yufu's hand.

The dark muzzle of Fei Yufu's gun was pointed at Grandpa Weisbu like a chilling eye.

Confused and shocked, Grandpa Weisbu trained his questioning eyes at Fei Yufu's.

Fei Yufu also fixed his muzzle-like chilling eyes at Grandpa Weisbu.

The muzzle looked like an eye!

Each eye looked like the muzzle!

"Fei Yufu, you…"

Grandpa Weisbu shivered all over, and his voice was senile and coarse.

He was baffled!

"Hahaha!" Tepiao suddenly burst into a guffaw as derisive as an owl's hoot. "You're confounded, right? Fei Yufu's the real 'Scorpion'! I'm the only one who knows."

"What?!" Grandpa screamed. He held out his hand, attempting to claw Fei Yufu's face, "…What a 'Scorpion' you are! You…you…you're really venomous!"

His held-out hand stayed immobile in the air.

Thud! He dropped to the ground.

The black horse Bamu neighed with shock.

The white horse Silu suddenly reared up.

"Huh huh—

Releasing a long neigh, Silu set about galloping along the path toward the outside of the forest like a hawk in flight, the small schoolbag swinging back and forth from its neck.

Fei Yufu was taken aback.

Looking up, he saw Gulong on the heaving back of the horse.

"Darn it! Gulong's getting away!" shouted Tepiao.

"What're you yelling for?" Fei Yufu said with reproach. He hurriedly got hold of the black horse Bumu, pushed Liu Bie's body off its back, and mounted into the saddle.

Fei Yufu stroked Bamu's crest and mane a few times before pulling the harness tight with the same hand and securely grasped the drug bag in the other.

"Good boy, Bamu! Hurry! Let's run after Silu, catch up with Silu!"

But Bamu's legs seemed to be pinned on the ground.

It would not budge.

Clinging to Grandpa Weisbu lying in the blood, it whinnied and wept.

Seeing Silu galloping out of sight, Fei Yufu grew anxious, sweat beginning to seep from his forehead.

He had not expected that Tepiao should have been more anxious than he was, screeching at the top of his lungs:

"Untie me quick! Untie me quick! When your horse runs, it'll drag me to my death."

Only then did Fei Yufu realize that Tepiao was still tied to the saddle.

Before Fei Yufu took action, Bamu burst into neighing.

By screeching, Tepiao unwittingly reminded the horse Bamu of his presence with the broad lotus-leaf-shaped face. Bamu adamantly believed him to be the murderer of Grandpa Weisbu.

Neighing and snorting angrily, it turned from side to side. It snaked its head around violently trying to bump and champ him; it bucked and reared, attempting to kick him.

Tepiao panicked and dodged desperately.

"Get me off…Get me off…"

Fei Yufu looked back and pulled the trigger—

Bang!

The bullet went into Tepiao's forehead.

Without uttering a whimper, Tepiao collapsed to the ground headfirst.

"Now, no one knows who I am."

With that, he fired another shot to cut Tepiao loose from the coir rope with the bullet.

"Bamu, Bamu, I've done away with the thug. Let's catch up with Silu. Let's hurry back to our checkpoint!"

He gave Bamu a few taps on its hips with his hand and a squeeze on its sides with his legs.

Lifting its head and neighing, Bamu darted off in the direction where Silu galloped out of sight.

Chapter 12

Carrying Gulong, Silu galloped on the forest path.

Grasping the reins, Gulong undulated on Silu's heaving back.

The report of the Fei Yufu's gunfire to kill Grandpa Weisbu had awakened him from unconsciousness

Lying low on the horseback, he had seen and heard everything.

He had abruptly lifted the reins and issued his secret command to charge forward.

He wanted to rush out of the forest and tell Uncle Ban Zhang about what he had seen and heard.

Fei Yufu is the "Scorpion"!

Fei Yufu is the "Scorpion"!

He repeated it in silence.

Silu was tearing along.

Against the strong wind, the schoolbag was slinging from its neck like a flapping palm leaf.

Trees rushed to the back one by one as swiftly as lightning.

Vines appeared in the front clumps after clumps like flying clouds.

Holding the reins tight, Gulong wished to have wings that could carry him swooshing out of the forest in an instant.

The forest was getting thinner and thinner in front of him.

The forest path was becoming wider and wider.

Ah! He was about to get out of the forest!

Out of it, the path would merge into a road leading to the checkpoint, a road with which Silu was the most familiar.

Victory was in sight!

But suddenly, suddenly! Gulong heard the "clip-clop-clip-clop" of a horse behind.

He looked back and saw Fe Yufu drawing nearer and nearer.

"On the double, Silu. Fast! Run fast!" commanded Gulong loudly as he pulled the reins tighter.

Silu galloped like mad.

The "clip-clop-clip-clop" behind sounded increasingly closer and louder.

Nevertheless, Gulong was confident.

He was confident that Silu could dash out of the forest in time.

He was confident that Silu could dart to the road before Fei Yufu could catch up.

Once out of the forest and onto the road, Fei Yufu would have to stop his chase.

It was because there would be traffic there.

Fei Yufu feared traffic; he feared people!

The confidence in triumph shot through his entire body bringing his blood, as it were, to a boil.

Fast! Fast!

Gulong had nothing on his mind but the one word "Fast!"

Gulong needed nothing but the one word "Fast!"

Rush out of the forest!

Rush onto the road!

Fast! Fast!

But just then—

Bang!

A gunshot sounded behind.

The bullet skimmed over Gulong's head.

Gulong broke out in a cold sweat.

Unable to catch up with Gulong, Fei Yufu was striking his vicious blows.

He must be afraid that I'll disclose his identity when I get to the checkpoint, Gulong was thinking.

He wants to hide his identify so he can continue his evil doings.

No way!

No way!

Gulong bit his teeth!

He would not see the blood of his loved ones shed for nothing!

He would tell the checkpoint head Ban Zhang that Fei Yufu was the "Scorpion" even at the cost of his own life.

He lay low with his head and chest pressed on the horse-back.

Bang!

Another shot.

This time, the bullet skimmed over his shoulders and punched a hole in the dangling schoolbag.

Gulong saw this shot as one that had hit him.

His eyes flared with anger.

What if Fei Yufu hits Silu…? He pondered.

What if Silu falls…?

Then everything will be over!

What to do?

What to do?

If he can't hit me, he'll fire at Silu for sure!

He suddenly thought of the blue cloth schoolbag. Fei Yufu had made it for him in a hurry before they had come out. He also remembered Fei Yufu placing it over Silu's neck at the farewell ceremony…

Now, it was the same Fei Yufu that had punched a big black hole through the bag.

"Yes, that's it!" Gulong got an idea, which, like a bulb, lit up his heart.

Gulong grabbed the bag and pulled it open to reveal its snow-white lining.

Pressed for time on the heaving back of his horse, Gulong could not afford any hesitation.

He bit his forefinger so that it bled.

The horse was galloping.

His hand was trembling.

His forefinger was bleeding.

On the back of the galloping horse, Gulong wrote on the schoolbag's snow-white lining with his trembling fore-finger—

Fei Yufu is the Scorpion.

After he finished, Guolong buttoned up the schoolbag and tapped Silu's neck and said:

"Silu, good boy Silu! You must run nonstop. Never stop. Run out of the forest and to the checkpoint.

Bang! Bang!

Gunshots sounded again.

Fei Yufu was aiming at Silu.

Without hesitation, Gulong let go the reins and rolled off Silu's back.

He fell into a thick growth of grass interspersed with small, fresh, yellow flowers.

Gunshots stopped.

Silu was shocked and balked.

It turned around and trotted toward Gulong.

It fixed its wide-open eyes at Gulong lying in the thick growth of grass.

Suddenly, it drew up its forearms and dropped to its knees.

It meant for Gulong to climb up its back.

It wanted to bring Gulong out of the forest.

"No!"

In an instant, tears welled up in Gulong's eyes.

"Hurry and get up, Silu. Get up quick!"

Gulong shouted hoarsely.

He turned his face aside, not having the heart to expose his teary eyes to Silu or looking into Silu's eyes filled with loyalty.

"Silu, leave me alone. Hurry and run! I got off because I wanted you to run faster. Go and run fast and deliver the schoolbag to the checkpoint as soon as you can."

He gave Silu a hard tap on its neck and a hard push on its croup.

This was his secret command for Silu to charge onward.

Silu suddenly lept into the air and dashed away as if carried by a pair of wings.

Like a cloud, a white cloud, it disappeared into the green distance.

Gulong rolled quickly into the thick growth of grass. Meanwhile, Fei Yufu whooshed by following the trail of Silu...

Chapter 13

A man was crawling on the meadow.

He had a gunshot wound on his bleeding leg.

He had inflicted the wound on himself.

Having failed to catch up with Silu, he had watched it galloping far away from him. Then, to his surprise, he had found Gulong missing on the horseback. However, he had had no time to give it too much thought. He had stopped chasing, led the black horse Bamu into the forest, and unloaded the bag of drugs.

He had concealed the bag and let go the horse Bamu. Then, he had aimed his gun at his leg and pulled the trigger.

He had thrown the gun into a muddy pond and was now crawling toward the checkpoint.

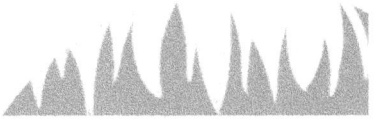

While pulling himself forward, he was fabricating his lies.

He would tell the head of the checkpoint Ban Zhang to send people in a hurry to encircle and annihilate the drug dealers and rescue their fellow guards.

He was thinking that Mangla, still hung from a tree, could be an eyewitness with the evidence of him battling with the drug dealers.

A smirk flashed on his chilling face.

However, he had never imagined that, right now, Ban Zhang was taking off Silu's neck the small schoolbag with a bullet hole in it.

Ban Zhang opened the bag and found to his astonishment a line of texts—

A line of texts written in blood!

First written in April 1983 in Kunming
Revised in April 2018 in Beijing

www.ingramcontent.com/pod-product-compliance
Lightning Source LLC
Chambersburg PA
CBHW041606240626
47164CB00009B/198